Bridesmaid Blues for Becky

The
Twelve Candles Club

1. *Becky's Brainstorm*
2. *Jess and the Fireplug Caper*
3. *Cara's Beach Party Disaster*
4. *Tricia's Got T-R-O-U-B-L-E!*
5. *Melanie and the Modeling Mess*
6. *Bridesmaid Blues for Becky*

Bridesmaid Blues for Becky

Elaine L. Schulte

BETHANY HOUSE PUBLISHERS
MINNEAPOLIS, MINNESOTA 55438

Published in association with the literary agency of Alive Communications, P.O. Box 49068, Colorado Springs, CO 80949.

Cover illustration by Andrea Jorgenson

Published by Bethany House Publishers
A Ministry of Bethany Fellowship, Inc.
11300 Hampshire Avenue South
Minneapolis, Minnesota 55438

Printed in the United States of America

Library of Congress Cataloging-in-Publication Data

Schulte, Elaine L.
Bridesmaid blues for Becky / Elaine L. Schulte
p. cm. — (The Twelve Candles Club ; #6)
Summary: When twelve-year-old Becky's mother plans to remarry, Becky and the youngest son of the groom join forces to stop the wedding.

[1. Remarriage—Fiction. 2. Family life—Fiction. 3. Christian life—Fiction.] I. Title. II. Series: Schulte, Elaine L. Twelve Candles Club ; 6.
PZ7.S3867Br 1994
[Fic]—dc20 94-19909
ISBN 1-55661-255-9 CIP
AC

To Barb Lilland, a super editor,

and to my other sisters and brothers at

Bethany House Publishers.

ELAINE L. SCHULTE is the well-known author of twenty-seven novels for women and children. Over one million copies of her popular books have been sold. She received a Distinguished Alumna Award from Purdue University as well as numerous other awards for her work as an author. A former Californian, she and her husband make their home in Austin, Texas, where she writes full time.

CHAPTER

1

At exactly four-thirty on Friday afternoon, Becky Hamilton leaned forward and announced, "This meeting of the Twelve Candles Club shall now come to order!"

She straightened the headband over her brown hair as she eyed the other four members: Tricia Bennett, Cara Hernandez, Melanie Lin, and Jess McColl. They jabbered on as they sat on the corner twin beds in Jess's room—all except Jess, who grunted as she worked out on her blue gymnastic mats.

Becky raised a hand to quiet everyone, but the chatter only grew louder. *They've made me president of the club, and now they won't listen,* she thought. This time she belted out an impatient, "O-r-d-e-r i-n t-h-e c-o-u-r-t!"

WHOA! What was she saying? Even Tumbles Burglar-Catcher McColl, Jess's new puppy, watched her.

The girls giggled—and stared at her.

Becky swallowed hard. It was all because of the secret she'd been keeping from them. She wiped her damp palms on the waist of her blue Tee and quickly corrected herself with another, "This meeting of the Twelve Candles Club—"

Grinning, Tricia blurted, "Order in the court? You wacko! *You* even have your T-shirt on backwards!" She flung back her reddish blond hair and gave a wild laugh, which wasn't surprising since she was their most dramatic member.

Becky slid her fingers around the neck of her shirt, and felt heat rush to her cheeks. The label *was* inside the front. She felt like running to Jess's bathroom to put her Tee on right, but she couldn't leave now!

Still laughing, Tricia gasped, "Becky Anne Hamilton, you're going even more wacko . . . if that's possible!"

Cara's brown eyes sparkled as she laughed and shook her thick wavy dark hair across the shoulders of her yellow Tee. She didn't seem shy now. "Becky *going* wacko? She's not *going*, she's gone! *Mucho* weird president of Club El Wacko!" Her secretary's notebook for the minutes of the meeting fell off her lap and she leaned over to get it, still laughing. Cara caught her breath long enough to choke out a "Shall I note the president's condition in the minutes?"

Melanie Lin, a petite, beautiful Asian-American model and their newest member, looked terrific in an orange Tee with white shorts. She laughed so merrily that her brown eyes were nearly hidden entirely.

Jess, their short and sturdy gymnast, stopped chuckling long enough to turn a perfect back flip on the gymnastic mat as if it were an exclamation point to their hilarity.

Not that Becky could complain about Jess. On weekdays the club met from four-thirty to five-thirty in her white high-ceilinged bedroom, which was really a three-car garage. It had been remodeled into a bedroom-gym that held Jess's gymnastic equipment, trophies, and prize ribbons. Most important, she had her own personal telephone and number, and she let the club use it.

Becky wished they'd stop acting so silly and laughing at her. She wished too that she could start the meeting—and plenty of other things in life—over.

"This meeting of the Twelve Candles Club shall *now* come to order!" she repeated loudly.

It didn't make any difference.

She got up from the oak desk chair, turned it around and sat down on it backwards (like her shirt), but even a more assertive stance didn't get their attention. "Come on, guys! P-l-e-a-s-e, let's come to order!"

"Phewww!" Jess answered, sobering down and plopping onto her blue gym matting. "I don't know why, but I feel so . . . crazy."

Melanie raised her dark brows. "Maybe something exciting is going to happen."

Becky ignored them. "Stop!" she yelled. "We're supposed to be twelve years old. And I thought we'd started this club to make money!"

Tricia stopped laughing and gave her a quizzical look. "What's gotten into you, Beck? You're not even dressed right!"

"I just want to get the business done before the phone starts ringing," she replied to avoid the real answer. "Will the secretary please read the minutes of the last meeting?"

Cara let out a deep breath, then read from her secretary's notebook, "At the last meeting, we accepted five new jobs. Becky signed up to baby-sit the Johnston girls tonight—"

"Oh no!" Becky broke in, her heart sinking. "I can't do

it. I just can't do it. Something important came up and I just plain forgot."

They all gazed at her. Probably they were thinking she'd always been so careful about writing her jobs in her daily planner . . . what was happening to her?

Sure enough, Tricia asked, "What came up?"

"Never mind," Becky answered. Then, for the first time in her life, her hands began to tremble, really tremble. She made her hands into fists to stop the shaking.

Suddenly everyone grew silent.

Cara was always the most sensitive one, and after a moment, she offered, "I'd be glad to baby-sit the Johnston kids for you. I need more money for school clothes next month anyhow."

"Thanks," Becky replied, hoping that would bring an end to their questions. No sense telling them what was happening in her life. Besides, she didn't want to think about it herself.

Jess went to the greenboard on the wall behind the desk, erased the white BECKY from the Johnston sitting job and chalked in CARA.

Cara read on from her secretary's report, but there were no other changes or details of importance.

That finished, Becky continued in her presidential tone, "May we have the treasurer's report?"

Tricia glanced at her curiously again, then opened her notebook. "As of today, Friday, July 18, there's $12.45 in the treasury, so we don't need to put in money for Morning Fun for Kids treats or anything else."

After that came old and new business, but there was nothing really new or exciting, not like there had been when the club had started. Tomorrow—Saturday—they'd wash cars, clean houses, and baby-sit. They never worked on Sundays, and Becky would be having a slumber party.

At four-forty the phone rang and Becky raced through, "If there's no further business, is there a motion that this meeting be adjourned?"

"I make a motion that this meeting be adjourned!" Jess shouted out.

"I second the motion!" Tricia put in quickly.

Cara picked up the ringing phone during Becky's it's-been-moved-and-seconded. "Twelve Candles Club," she said into the mouthpiece. "May we help you?"

She listened for a while, and Becky thought that if she drew a picture of Cara right now, she would look wide-eyed and perplexed. Still on the phone, Cara turned to Becky. "Just a moment while I ask them, Mrs. Llewellyn."

She put her hand over the phone and said, "It's Mrs. L. . . . and you know she never wants us to discuss her jobs and have us phone her back like we do everyone else."

They all liked Mrs. Llewellyn, even if she was eccentric and tried to avoid their client-call-back rule.

"Well, working for her is always an adventure," Tricia remarked with a shrug.

"And who knows what kind of a party Mrs. L. might be giving next?" Becky put in.

"We can waive the rule for her," Jess said.

"You're sure?" Becky asked.

"I'm sure," Jess answered. "After all, she helped us get the club started."

Almost together, they nodded in acceptance.

Cara's hand was still over the phone's receiver, and she eyed Becky strangely. "Mrs. L. wants to know if we can work next

Saturday night . . . for an *engagement* party for your mother and Mr. Bradshaw. . . ."

Becky's heart stopped.

All of them watched her, including Tumbles Burglar-Catcher McColl, who gave a bark.

"Your mom's engaged?!" Tricia exclaimed. "Well . . . *no wonder* you're acting so weird. Why didn't you tell us?"

Becky shook her head and stared at the blue floor mat. Now she had to discuss it, like it or not.

"Guess I was hoping it wasn't really true . . . or they'd change their minds . . . or . . . something," she mumbled.

"When did you find out?" Cara asked.

"Last week I started to guess what was happening. Only Mr. Bradshaw can be sort of a joker and keep you off balance," Becky told them. "But last night he was over for dinner, and he and Mom announced it to Gram and Amanda and me."

"*It?*" Tricia asked. "Meaning that they're going to get married?"

Becky nodded. "They were happy as could be . . . everyone except me." Just as fast as she'd spoken, she wished her words had stayed hidden inside.

"Mr. Bradshaw seems like a nice man, Beck," Jess said in her reasonable tone. "Besides, he's got tons of money. And aren't you the one who was trying to get your mother to marry him just last month?"

"I was desperate then," Becky explained. "Now Mom has a super job, and we're beginning to do just fine with it and my earnings from the Twelve Candles Club. We were all right . . . anyhow, starting to be all right on our own."

"Then why?" Jess asked, eager as always to get to the bottom of things. "Why are they getting married?"

Becky blew out a discouraged breath. "They say they're in l-o-v-e, really and truly in l-o-v-e. And they've decided they wanted to go on the Israel trip with our church next month for a honeymoon, so they've hurried everything up—"

"Yipes!" Jess said. "I hadn't told you yet, but I just found out I may be going with my whole family on the Israel trip."

"Me, too, maybe," Melanie put in. She looked at Becky with amazement. "Don't tell me your mom and Mr. Bradshaw are taking you along on their honeymoon!"

"No way!" Becky replied. "Absolutely no way would I even go with them—"

They heard Mrs. Llewellyn squawking impatiently on the phone, and Cara crossed her eyes. "I forgot!"

"Just one more moment, Mrs. L.," she said into the phone. She listened, then added, "Oh, yes, you always pay very well. We just need another minute to work things out. It's a little . . . ummmm . . . complicated. Are you sure that we can't call you back?"

Everyone heard Mrs. L. squawk what sounded like, "I'll wait, dear, till you work out your complications. Tell Becky that—" The rest of Mrs. L.'s words were impossible to understand.

"Just one more moment then, please." Cara put the phone against the stomach of her yellow T-shirt. "Mrs. L. says you wouldn't be expected to work, Beck . . . that you'll be one of the honored guests."

Cara paced with the phone, waiting for them to decide.

"Look, do you want us to work at the engagement party or not?" Tricia asked Becky. "It's your mother, but you know Mrs. L. She's given us lots of work ever since the beginning of the club."

Becky lifted her shoulders and dropped them hopelessly. "Someone has to do it, so *you* may as well be the ones. Besides, it'd really look strange if you turned down this party."

She wasn't sure how she felt about being a guest at the party. Maybe she'd suddenly get sick. No, Mom would see through that. Probably she'd have to go. So much for being "honored"!

She listened as Cara spoke into the phone. "Yes, we'd be glad to take the party-helper job, Mrs. Llewellyn. Shall we wear our cowgirl outfits or—Oh yes, the white skirts and blouses and the candle medallions. Okay, it's set. Saturday from five to eleven. We always appreciate working for you. Thank you very much for asking us."

Yeah, thanks a lot! Becky thought.

It was bad enough that she and Amanda, her five-year-old sister, had to go to a "special dinner tonight to become better acquainted with Mr. Bradshaw's sons." As it was, his college-aged "boys" always seemed to treat her and Amanda like pests. And now to have to go to the engagement party Mrs. Llewellyn was giving for Mom and Mr. Bradshaw! It was too much.

Becky saw her friends' faces cloud with worry, and she decided not to act as unhappy as she felt. Maybe she should pretend—just pretend—to be unaffected by "the big news."

After Cara hung up, the phone started ringing madly, one call after another, and Becky was glad she didn't have to discuss Mom and Mr. Bradshaw further. All she wanted was for someone—maybe even God—to s-t-o-p t-h-e w-e-d-d-i-n-g!

CHAPTER

2

When the four of them left the meeting, Cara headed across the street from Jess's for her own house. "See you," she called out with a worried glance at Becky.

Becky just nodded and let Tricia and Melanie do the answering for her. She glanced down at the sidewalk, feeling a lot like crying. As it was, she'd already discussed more about Mom's engagement and the upcoming wedding than she'd like. If only this hadn't—

"There's your mom coming home from work now," Tricia said as they walked along.

Becky glanced ahead.

Mom was driving their green Oldsmobile into the driveway, and the top of five-year-old Amanda's head poked up from the front passenger seat. They were eight or nine houses away now, far enough away that maybe they hadn't seen her. And their garage door was opening, so she wouldn't have to face them for a few minutes.

Better yet, Mr. Bradshaw's car wasn't in their driveway . . . which meant he wouldn't be out trimming the overgrown bushes in front of the house like he'd offered last night.

Dumb thought! Of course he wouldn't be coming tonight, since he was cooking dinner for them at his house.

Melanie shook her head to fluff out her cloud of dark hair, maybe because it was a hot day. "It must be exciting for your mom to be getting married again," she remarked. "I don't know how I'd feel about it, though. I suppose I just can't imagine my mom marrying any man except my father."

Becky grimaced. "Me neither," she mumbled.

She couldn't stop thinking about her father, who had been killed two years ago in a freeway wreck. *Oh, Daddy! Why did you have to leave us?* she thought miserably. It seemed just a month or two ago, Mom had said she still loved him. How could she be so fickle? Then a terrible idea hit, and Becky's heart hurt at the thought: *Maybe Mom had never really loved Dad at all!*

"I said, what's Mr. Bradshaw like?" Melanie was asking.

Becky shrugged. "All right, I guess. Last night, he tried to lighten things up by telling Amanda and me riddles and knock-knock jokes."

"You're kidding," Tricia said. "Like what?"

Becky racked her brain, then remembered one. "What do you say if a cat bites you?"

"I give up," Tricia said. "What?"

"Me O-w."

"Ufffff," Melanie responded, shaking her hair again. "Sounds exactly like something my brother William would come up with. Let's hear another."

Becky remembered one more. "Knock-knock."

"Who's there?" Tricia asked.

"Dogs."

"Dogs who?" Melanie asked.

Becky rolled her eyes. "No, they don't. Owls do."

When they didn't get it, she added, "Dogs don't w-h-o. Owls h-o-o."

"Got it," Tricia said, rolling her eyes hopelessly.

Melanie gave a laugh. "Ooooooooooooo! At least he must be trying to make friends with you . . . or something."

"Amanda loves it," Becky told them, then kicked at a big leaf on the sidewalk. "I guess his three sons must think he's hilarious. But Mr. Bradshaw already admitted that he doesn't know much about girls or girl stuff."

"And you probably don't know much about boys or boy stuff," Melanie said. "Believe me, brothers are different, and sometimes they can be a pain."

"Don't tell me!" Becky said. "I don't want to hear it." *Boys are definitely a pain,* she thought. *They just get in the way. Jess's big brothers always tease her, and Melanie's little brother always plays dumb jokes.*

She watched as Mom's car pulled into their driveway up ahead. *You shouldn't make me live with those Bradshaw boys,* her thoughts pleaded silently with Mom. *It's not fair! I've never had brothers, and I'm not ready to start now! Besides, we'd be outnumbered . . . three of them, and only two of us.*

"Well, at least you won't have to move clear across the country," Tricia said brightly. "Remember when you thought you'd be moving to Omaha or Colorado Springs or . . . I can't even remember all the places your mom was checking out for you to move to a few months ago."

"Well, it's almost as bad," Becky answered, tears filling her eyes. She looked away and blinked hard. "It sounds like we'll have to move to Mr. Bradshaw's house on Seaview Boulevard." She didn't even want to think that she might have to go to a new school, at least try it for a semester.

"It's not fair," Melanie objected, "your having to move when I've just gotten to know you!"

Becky nodded silently.

"I guess your moving to his house makes sense, though," Tricia was saying thoughtfully, even though they'd been next-door friends since their playpen days. "It's a lot bigger house, and with his three sons, there'd be five kids in the family. Including your mom and Mr. Bradshaw, that's seven!"

But I don't want to move! I don't want to leave Tricia, and all my friends in Santa Rosita Estates! Suddenly, Becky's head filled with fearful thoughts. *Once I move away, things will never be the same. Their lives will go on without me here, and I'll be way over there on the other side of town, and I'll almost never see them, and the Twelve Candles Club and everything will be ruined! My whole life is ruined!*

Tricia let out a loud "Whoa!" then laughed. "You'd live next door to the one-and-only Mrs. Llewellyn! That'd be a change from living next to me!"

Becky asked huffily, "You think Mrs. L. would turn into my best friend, like you?"

Tricia's grin faded. "No way!"

They were silent for an instant before Melanie said, "I'm dying to meet Mrs. L. at the party Saturday tonight. She sounds almost as eccentric as my Auntie Ying-Ying."

As they neared Tricia's house, Melanie said, "Well . . . see you!"

"Yeah, see you," Becky answered with Tricia.

Melanie gave a little wave, then headed for her two-story white house behind what she called "the great wall of China" on the cul-de-sac.

Walking on with Tricia, Becky remarked, "I guess Melanie's family will be discussing Mom getting remarried. Probably right at dinner. In fact, I bet *everyone's* family will be discussing it. Maybe your mother already knows, with her being Mom's best friend."

"Could be," Tricia answered, "but she didn't tell me. She's good at keeping secrets."

"Jess's mom isn't," Becky said. She felt sure Mrs. McColl, who was a realtor, would air the news all over Santa Rosita Estates. Cara's mother was quieter, but she worked a lot at the Hernandez family's video store, Flicks, so she'd probably add to the neighborhood news broadcast.

Tricia had stopped on the sidewalk in front of her peach-colored, two-story house, her eyes full of concern. "I guess you feel bad because of your dad. But Mom's aunt got married three months after her husband's funeral. Three months, not two years like your mom! He proposed to her right after the funeral. It would have been a scandal, but they were all good friends . . . and old, too, I guess."

Becky decided not to answer, and Tricia finally asked, "Is there anything I can do to help, Beck?"

Becky clamped her jaws together, then shook her head. "Nope." She definitely did not want to go home, but standing on the sidewalk wouldn't help matters. "See you tomorrow."

"I'm going to pray for you," Tricia stated firmly. "That's what I can do."

Becky blinked her eyes hard again, then looked away. "I guess so."

"You want to come in and talk more about it?"

"No way," Becky answered.

"You're going to have to face this," Tricia warned.

Instead of answering, Becky turned and made her way slowly to the sidewalk of her small white Spanish-style house. The last thing she wanted was to discuss her problems. As for facing them, she sure wasn't ready. It was impossible, that's all. And her friends would probably be asking endless questions at her slumber party Sunday night.

As she let herself in the front door, a new thought hit. Maybe tonight at the so-called "family dinner" with Mr. Bradshaw and his sons, a wild and wonderful idea would come to her, just like the brainstorm for the Twelve Candles Club had come during her birthday party. Maybe God would flash a great idea into her brain about how to s-t-o-p t-h-e w-e-d-d-i-n-g.

"Becky!" her five-year-old sister, Amanda, called out from the living room. "Here's Becky!"

"Hi, Amanda-Panda," Becky answered dully. She closed the front door behind her more loudly than she'd intended.

"You mad?" Amanda asked.

Becky shrugged, then realized that was part of how she felt. Mad-mad-mad-mad. Sad-sad-sad-sad. Mad and sad all together, that was it.

"Gram got me dressed," Amanda informed her, showing off her yellow and white butterfly sundress. She wore a perky yellow bow in her brown hair and lacy white socks and her new white sandals.

"It looks like Gram's special touches," Becky answered.

Gram was an interior decorator and lived near the ocean,

and this summer, she often baby-sat Amanda after preschool. Gram claimed that Amanda looked just like their mother had when she was five: thick dark brown hair, dark eyelashes, big blue eyes, and just plump enough to look cuddly and innocent.

"We're going to Mr. Bradshaw's house," Amanda announced in her very-important voice. Buster Bunny, the brown stuffed rabbit Mr. Bradshaw had given her, was clutched under her arm. "Mom said you should wear your blue sundress that matches mine."

"My *blue* sundress?" Becky objected, as if she might own another summer dress.

Amanda nodded. "We're going to meet his boys."

Becky objected again. "His *boys*! They're all grown up, either in high school or college. They're almost men, or maybe they are already."

"Well, he called them 'his boys,' " Amanda argued, not at all flustered. "He said his 'boys' would be there for dinner tonight. That's what he said. I 'member."

Becky didn't want to fight about it. She made her way through the small white living room. As she passed the sliding glass door to the backyard, their old collie, Lass, looked up at them from in front of her dog house. Becky hurried outside to give Lass a big hug.

"What will happen to you, girl?" Becky whispered as she held her tight. "What will happen to you now? Probably Mr. Bradshaw will say you're too old to keep with them . . . or some other excuse since they have a dog, too."

Lass only licked her face.

When she came back in, Becky glanced through the dining area toward the strangely silent kitchen. "Where's Mom?"

"In her room," Amanda reported. "She's on the phone with

Mr. Bradshaw. And, after that, we're not supposed to bother her. She's gonna take a nice l-o-n-g bubble bath."

"Hmmmph!" Becky answered. Before Mr. Bradshaw came into their lives, Mom would have been rushing around in the kitchen . . . maybe cooking a pizza or spaghetti or something that made the whole house smell good. Lately the house smelled empty . . . as if they didn't even have a kitchen in it, except when Mom cooked for *Mister* Bradshaw.

She'd no more than thought it than she realized the house smelled like rolls baking. The next moment, the oven buzzer went off, blaring through the house.

Mom stuck her head into the hallway from her bedroom. "Becky, could you take the poppyseed rolls from the oven? After they're cool, put them in the basket on the counter . . . then get out the leftover carrot cake so we don't forget to take it with us."

"Okay."

Becky trudged to the kitchen.

The flowered oven mitts were already out, so she pulled them on, then opened the oven. The golden rolls with the black poppyseeds sprinkled on top looked done and smelled wonderful. She took them from the oven and set them on the stove.

From the refrigerator, she took out the foil-topped pan of leftover carrot cake—a grim reminder of last night's dinner. Did the Bradshaw sons know the "big news" yet? she wondered. And if so, what would they say?

Finally, she headed down the hallway for her room and, sure enough, heard Mom's voice on the phone. It sounded soft and lovey.

How can you talk like that with Mr. Bradshaw when Dad

died only two years ago? Becky thought. *How can you forget Dad? How can you?*

Amanda followed right behind her. She lowered her voice. "You want to listen at her bedroom door like we used to?"

"No way! No way do I want to hear—" She stopped just in time, or she'd have said, "Mom talking mushy."

Amanda's blue eyes widened. "We listened other times. Why can't we—"

"Well, we're not going to now. Besides, that was only when she talked to Mrs. Bennett about us."

Amanda's voice filled with disappointment. "Don't you think they're talking about us?"

"They don't even care about us now!"

She felt like adding a harsh, *Now leave me alone!* but Amanda's face was scrunching up, and she was beginning to look as uncertain as Becky. Bad news, because Amanda might cry . . . really howl out loud . . . then tell Mom what they'd been discussing.

"Come on," Becky told her. "You can bring Buster Bunny to my room. Tell me what you and Gram did today."

Amanda brightened. "Gram and I went to the beach, and we went shopping, and . . ."

Becky scarcely heard the rest of it. Instead, she listened as Mom hung up the phone and started running water into the bathtub.

Since when did Mom take long bubble baths?!

Since now!

Just after six o'clock, Mom arrived in the living room wearing a new silky black and white dress that made her look even more slim. She gave a little modeling twirl, and the dress whirled around her knees. "I bought the dress at lunchtime. How do I look?"

"Nice," Amanda said right away.

"Fine," Becky answered more slowly, even though her mother looked wonderful. Instead of having her dark hair pulled back in a barrette, as usual, she'd done it all up in a French twist. She wore her big white earrings and white high-heeled shoes. Her blue-green eyes sparkled with excitement. She looked way too happy, not to mention way too beautiful.

Mom tucked her small white purse under her arm. "Let's hurry so we're not late. We wouldn't want to be responsible for Paul ruining dinner—"

Did Mom have to say his name in such a mushy way? Becky thought, backing away.

"Aren't you ready?" Mom asked her.

"I have to get something from my room." Anything so she wouldn't have to face the evening. Anything to delay.

"Hurry it up then," Mom answered, still smiling. "We'll wait in the car out in the garage for you."

Becky trudged down the hallway to her room and shut the door behind her.

She'd not only have to move to Mr. Bradshaw's house—but give up her room—this room. She stared around it, heartsick. It was perfect, with white furniture, powder blue carpet and lots of blue, white, and yellow accents. The corner twin beds were covered with powder blue comforters with big yellow and white daisies on them, and matching pillows. It was a perfect room, at least in her artistic judgment.

She turned away and glimpsed herself in the full-length mirror behind the door. Not so artistically perfect, but fine:

her brown wavy hair was held down by a white headband, and her tall, gangly body was half-hidden in her blue sundress with the tiny white butterfly print. The sundress made her look as if she were going to Sunday school or to a summer party . . . instead of heading for certain doom.

She puffed her cheeks out at herself. "Get going, Becky!" she said. "Get going before you're in even more trouble!"

Finally, she made her way through the house and out to the garage. She climbed into the car and buckled up with Amanda in the backseat.

"What'd you do in the house?" Amanda asked.

"Nothing," Becky answered. It was true if you didn't count looking in the mirror . . . and trying to delay what was happening to them.

"You did nothing?" Amanda exclaimed.

Luckily, Mom was so busy backing the car out of the garage and onto the street that she didn't seem to hear. They'd just started driving forward when she stepped on the brake. "Oh no! I almost forgot the poppyseed rolls and the carrot cake. Becky, could you—"

Becky unbuckled her seat belt. "I'm going."

Inside the house, she headed for the kitchen. She quickly piled the warm rolls in the basket, put a white napkin over them, and stacked the basket on the foil-topped pan of carrot cake.

When she arrived outside again, Tricia's mother had driven up in her maroon minivan and was talking through her van window to Mom in the car.

As Becky made her way toward them, Mrs. Bennett said, "Libby, I'm so very happy for you. Your life is turning into a whole new adventure—"

Uff! Becky thought as she set the cake pan on the curb. She jerked the back car door open so angrily, it knocked the basket of poppyseed rolls onto the street.

Yipes!

Glancing in the car, she saw that only Amanda had noticed.

Becky put a warning finger to her lips, then scooped up the poppyseed rolls from the asphalt and tucked them back into the basket. Luckily they didn't look dirty, maybe because the poppyseeds were as black as the asphalt street.

"Ready?" Mom asked as Becky settled back into her seat.

"Ready," Becky answered. The cake pan was between her and Amanda, and the basket was settled against the seat to prevent any more disasters.

As they drove through Santa Rosita Estates, Becky wondered again about how many neighbors had heard "the big news." Probably everyone had by now.

Driving along, Mom remarked, "I hear the Twelve Candles Club is going to help serve at Mrs. Llewellyn's engagement party for Paul and me."

"Yeah," Becky answered. "How did you know?"

"Mrs. L. phoned me at my office just before I left work," Mom answered. She glanced at Becky in the rearview mirror. "I'm so glad you're being so agreeable about everything, Beck."

Agreeable?! Becky wanted to yell, but something kept her from it. Maybe because Mom seemed so happy . . . or maybe because this seemed so unreal.

"It'll be wonderful for you and Amanda to be part of a big family and to live in the Bradshaw house," Mom said. "Tonight you'll see how cozy it actually is for such a big place."

Becky decided the Bradshaw dinner would be the perfect

chance to let everyone know *exactly* how she felt about the whole mess. On the other hand, the Bradshaw boys' mother had died just last year of cancer, and some of them might feel unhappy about the romance, too. Maybe, just maybe, between them something could be done yet.

Before long, they were driving down Seaview Boulevard, which had big pine trees and petunias in the street divider. The houses weren't in a development like Santa Rosita Estates. Seaview Boulevard houses were farther apart and all different—custom-built. A few were ultra-modern, like Mrs. Llewellyn's, and a lot were old Spanish style with red-tiled roofs.

Becky glanced through the pine trees and recognized the Bradshaw house. It did look friendlier than the others—the only weathered gray shake house, and it had an old-fashioned front porch with a swing and two rocking chairs on it. But friendly house or not, she was *not* going to like it!

As for this dinner with the Bradshaw "boys," she knew she would definitely not like it, either. In fact, she wasn't going to like anything if she could help it.

Her eyes filled with tears, but her heart hurt too much to let them run down her face.

CHAPTER

3

Standing on the porch of the Bradshaw house, Mom rang the doorbell. She held the foil-topped carrot cake, and turned to Becky and Amanda. "I expect you girls to behave," she stated firmly.

"I'll be good!" Amanda promised, smiling.

Becky took a deep breath, inhaling the poppyseed roll smell, since she held the basket in her hands. Her best hope was that the Bradshaw "boys" wouldn't want their father to get married, either.

Mr. Bradshaw threw the door open and stood there. Beside him, a small white dog with huge brown spots gave a bark, then began to wag his tail. A terrier, Mom had called him. If she sketched him, Becky thought, he'd look like a cartoon dog.

"Well . . . Libby . . . don't you look lovely?" Mr. Bradshaw said, as if he'd never seen her dressed up. It wasn't a real question, though. Judging by the look in his gray-blue eyes, he thought she was the most beautiful person on earth.

Finally he turned to Amanda and Becky. "Hello, girls . . . you're both looking very, very nice, too. But, then, how can you help it when you have such a beautiful mother?"

Instead of meeting his eyes, Becky glanced down at Amanda, who was beaming happily at him.

Her little sister might be impressed by his words, but Becky Hamilton was not going to give in.

She'd seen him long enough, though, to know he was looking nice with his short blond-gray hair, neatly trimmed beard and mustache. She guessed he was handsome for an older man. He wore his blue and yellow sport shirt with a white collar again, and white pants and shoes.

He'd worn the shirt the first day of the Twelve Candles Club's existence, when they'd stopped by to ask for work, and he'd told them about Mrs. Llewellyn. That time, it'd seemed comforting to see he liked yellow and blue, too. Today it didn't make her feel a bit better.

"Girls, our dog's name is Bullwinkle," Mr. Bradshaw announced, which made the dog wag his tail. "He loves being called by name. We've decided it makes him think he's the center of attention."

"Hi, Bullwinkle," Amanda said. She gave the dog a hesitant pat on his head, then another. "Hi, Bullwinkle!"

Next, Bullwinkle came to Becky, probably for a pat, too. She pretended not to see him, and she wasn't about to "Hi, Bullwinkle" him, either.

"Becky, where are your manners?" Mom asked.

"I—I was just thinking," Becky answered. She glanced at the porch swing quickly. "I was hoping that maybe we could sit on the swing."

"Maybe later," Mom said. She put her arm around Becky and gently eased her through the front door. "Come along now."

"Mom, don't!" Becky whispered.

"Don't what?"

Becky shook her head. *Don't push me into his house . . . don't be like this . . . don't change things . . . don't ruin our lives!* was what she wanted to say, but he'd hear.

Inside, the gray entry hall was big, and one wall was covered with red brick. Becky glanced into the living room. It was painted a dull gray, except for its reddish brick fireplace. Exactly the gloomy kind of place where Mr. Bradshaw's first wife could have died, Becky decided. It was definitely not the kind of place that Becky Hamilton wanted to live in.

Mr. Bradshaw must have read her mind since he said, "Afraid it looks sort of dreary. I've hired your Gram to come and lighten things up all over the house."

"Gram?!" Becky asked.

"Your mother and I thought she'd be the best decorator," he answered. "After all, she knows all of you well."

Becky didn't say a word.

For an instant, he looked disappointed, then he turned to Mom with the beginnings of a grin. "I'm making stir-fry, as promised, so we can all visit in the kitchen while I cook."

"Sounds like fun!" Mom said, enthusiastic. She led the way past the stairs and down a gray hallway that brought them to the kitchen. "The house already smells good."

"I'm making shrimp egg rolls for us to snack on while we cook," he explained. "They'll be ready in a few minutes."

Becky followed reluctantly, knowing that Mr. Bradshaw

was right behind her. Bullwinkle was also behind her, sniffing at her ankles.

As they stepped into the dark kitchen, Mr. Bradshaw turned to Becky. "Your Gram's hiring contractors to put in more windows, new lighting, white tile counters, and clay-colored floors. She came over this morning. She's going to change the whole house into a bright, cheerful place."

Becky didn't answer. *How can Gram let me down, too?* she thought. It sounded as if Gram was all for Mom marrying Mr. Bradshaw now, when last night she'd seemed as surprised as Becky.

Mom headed for the refrigerator with the leftover carrot cake as though she knew the kitchen well. "It's a roomy kitchen already," she added. "With all of the changes, it's going to be absolutely perfect, the most beautiful kitchen ever."

Who cares? Becky thought.

She glanced at the oven, since the light was on. Two trays of egg rolls were cooking, all right. She only wished they didn't smell so good and that she didn't feel hungry right now.

"I see you've been busy chopping," Mom remarked to Mr. Bradshaw. She nodded at the kitchen island, where a big stainless steel wok stood. Beside it, a huge chopping board held piles of cut-up chicken, carrots, celery, mushrooms, and all kinds of green vegetables.

"I sure have," he admitted. "I've got the rice going in the rice cooker, too."

The doorbell chimed, sounding low and melodious. Immediately Bullwinkle gave a yip.

"That must be your mother," he said to Mom in a pleased tone. "If you'll excuse me, I'll get the door—"

The moment he left, Mom said, "Becky, you could be a

bit more friendly to him. He really wants to please us so much."

Becky plopped the basket of poppyseed rolls on the island counter. "If he really wants to please me, then he could leave us the way we are."

Mom's face drooped with disappointment. "Oh, Becky, can't you *try* to be more accepting—"

Gram bustled into the kitchen. "I see everyone's here already," she chirped happily. "It's a wonderful family kitchen. . . ." Smiling at Becky and Amanda, she gave each of them a hug. She even greeted Bullwinkle by name and gave him a friendly pat, which made him wag his tail even harder. "It's going to be a wonderful family, isn't it?"

"Gram!" Becky muttered.

Gram didn't seem to notice. Instead, she started talking about the new ovens, range, and windows. She wore her soft blue-green dress, the same color of her eyes, and her short brown hair was neatly curled, perfectly in place.

She pulled a paint color folder from her purse and started showing different shades of off-white against the green walls. Everyone claimed Gram was a great interior designer and, when she was excited like this, she looked extra pretty. The only trouble was she seemed more interested in decorating Mr. Bradshaw's house than she was in stopping the wedding.

Finally, they decided on antique white for the main color. "Easy to remember, an 'antique' like me," Mr. Bradshaw laughed.

Mom shook her head, her eyes sparkling. "You seem like a rather young fella to me, Paul Bradshaw."

Urk! Becky thought.

Gram asked, "Do you have any new thoughts on the decorating, Paul?"

Grinning, he put his arm around Mom's shoulders. "So far, everything you've suggested sounds great to me. I'll leave it to Libby. You can do whatever she wants."

How could they be so urky? Becky thought.

Then as if matters weren't bad enough, Mom gave Mr. Bradshaw a lovey glance.

He must have noticed Becky's unhappiness, because he quickly let loose of Mom. Just then, the oven timer began to blare, too. "This young fella better not burn the egg rolls."

As he opened the oven, Mom glared at Becky. It was definitely a you'd-better-behave-young-lady look.

Becky plopped down on one of the bar stools by the cooking island. It appeared that she was stuck-stuck-stuck-stuck here . . . at least for now.

The steaming egg rolls were no more than set out on the kitchen island when Mr. Bradshaw's three sons came thundering down the steps from upstairs.

Oh no! Here we go. . . .

"Boys," he said, "I'm sure you remember Becky and Amanda from the time we went to dinner together last winter."

"Sure," answered Jonathan, the oldest. He was twenty-two years old—not to mention tall, almost blond, and so handsome Becky began to stare at him. He was going to college to be a lawyer, but he didn't sound brainy as he added, "Hi, ladies. How are you?"

The others added their greetings, and Becky just nodded. While Mr. Bradshaw introduced Gram to them, Becky looked over the other two Bradshaw "boys."

Charlie was shorter and twenty years old. He looked like a

Charlie—friendly with light brown curly hair.

But Quinn, who would be a senior in high school this year, was a different matter. Tall, skinny, and dark-haired, he'd trailed in behind them and eyed her family suspiciously from behind gold wire glasses. Quinn was definitely unfriendly.

Well, I'm not so sure I like you, either, Becky thought.

"I'll put Bullwinkle out in the backyard," he announced.

"Why?" Mr. Bradshaw asked. "Bullwinkle's in his element with so many people around."

But Quinn was already marching Bullwinkle out.

The rest of them talked and scarfed down the shrimp egg rolls while Mr. Bradshaw cooked the stir-fry in the wok. When Quinn came back in, Becky was glad he didn't talk much, either; he looked pleased with himself, though, as if he were up to something secret.

Finally it was time to go to the dining room table, and Becky brought in the basket of poppyseed rolls. Mr. Bradshaw sat down at one end of the table and Mom at the other—as if they were already their real parents.

Once everyone else was settled, Mr. Bradshaw bowed his head and said grace. It wasn't just thanking for food, but asking God that everyone would be glad and understanding about "our big news."

Becky felt certain Jonathan, Charlie, and Quinn already knew the "big news," too. She added a "P.S." to Mr. Bradshaw's grace, silently reminding God to please stop the wedding soon!

Next, Mr. Bradshaw began to serve rice and stir-fry onto the stack of plates before him—as if he were the father of the entire family. Just as bad, Mom was acting like everyone's mother, passing the soy sauce, and the rolls and butter.

Once everyone was served, Becky wondered if Mr. Bradshaw would tell jokes or dumb knock-knock stories again. Instead, he said, "Becky, why don't you tell my boys about the Twelve Candles Club?"

"About the Twelve Candles Club?!"

Mom shot her a warning glance, and Becky knew she'd better be agreeable, at least about this. "Well . . . there are five of us in the club, and we're all twelve years old. We do light housecleaning, car and window washing, baby-sitting, and party helping . . . all kinds of odd jobs. We also have Morning Fun for Kids, a daycare for kids four to eight years old on Monday, Wednesday, and Friday mornings—"

Suddenly Amanda screamed fearfully and climbed up onto her chair. She pointed at the table in front of her. "*A snake!* There's a snake right here!"

Mom jumped up from her chair, shrieking. "Paul, it's a snake!"

Becky leaped from her chair herself.

Mr. Bradshaw hurried over to protect them, yelling angrily, "Quinn, get that snake of yours out of here this minute! How did it get out of your room?"

Quinn ambled around the table to pick up the yellow and brown snake that was coiling itself around the stir-fry pot. A long black forked tongue flicked out and back into its mouth. "It's just a harmless python. Aren't you, Julius Squeezer?"

Becky couldn't stand to watch as he gathered up the long, squirmy snake and held it in big loops around his hands. *UGH!*

"So that's why you put Bullwinkle outside!" his father said, angry. "Did you really think you'd fool us? Go and put Julius out in your mother's potting shed right now. And be sure to let Bullwinkle back in. Now!"

Smirking, Quinn headed for the kitchen door with the snake in his hands.

"Paul, why didn't you tell me Quinn had a snake?" Mom asked.

"I was going to when it seemed the right time," he assured her, embarrassed. "I've been after Quinn to give it away or sell it back to the pet store."

Finally, they all sat down at the table again, Mr. Bradshaw still comforting Mom and Amanda. *One thing's sure,* Becky decided with a shudder. *I am not going to live in a house with a snake in it!*

Before long, Bullwinkle raced in. Except for Becky, they were all eating again when Quinn returned to the table.

As he sat down, Quinn took a deep breath and pushed his glasses back. "Contrary to popular belief, snakes are one of the finest animals on earth," he announced. "They never harm anyone except to protect themselves or their young, and they're highly intelligent pets. What's more, they are *not* slimy."

"That's enough, Quinn," his father warned. "That's quite enough for tonight."

Quinn had buttered his poppyseed roll, and now he bit into it. A peculiar expression raced across his face, and he carefully removed the bite of roll from his mouth. "Glass! There's glass in this roll!"

"Glass?" Jonathan repeated.

"She's trying to kill us!" Quinn declared, staring at Mom.

"Kill you?" she asked, her eyes wide. "Why on earth would anyone want to—"

"Who else would want us out of the way?" Quinn persisted.

Beside him, Charlie was taking a bite of roll from his mouth, too. He examined it carefully. "I don't think it's glass," he mused. "It looks more like stones . . . little stones mixed in with the poppyseeds—"

Suddenly everyone was inspecting their rolls, including Becky. It looked like bits of . . . asphalt from the street mixed with the poppyseeds. She began to have a terrible tight feeling in her stomach. Even worse than seeing the snake.

"Becky did it!" Amanda piped. "Becky dropped the rolls right on the street in front of our house, and then . . . and then . . . and then, without cleaning them off, she just put them back in the basket."

Everyone was staring at her. "I didn't mean to!" Becky protested. "I didn't mean to drop the rolls! Besides, only three fell on the street and they looked all right; so I just put them back in the basket. . . ."

Mr. Bradshaw gave a strangled laugh.

"Well, Libby," he said, "is it what you expected tonight?"

Mom gave a laugh too, then suddenly they were laughing together, laughing and laughing until they had Bullwinkle barking with excitement.

Gram and Charlie and Jonathan began to laugh with them as if they understood, and Amanda rolled her eyes back and forth, looking like maybe it was important for her to join in.

"What's so funny?" Quinn demanded into the racket.

Becky looked down in embarrassment.

Between laughs, Mr. Bradshaw gasped, "We were expecting resistance to our wedding announcement, but we didn't expect critters in the stir-fry and grime in the dinner rolls!"

He finally stopped to catch his breath, then began to chuckle again. "This is going to be some . . . some kind of

. . . an interesting family, isn't it!"

Bullwinkle gave a peculiar bark, as if in agreement.

"Ohhhhhhh!" Mom answered, laughing and holding her cheeks. Her eyes glistened. "It's turned out to be a dinner we'll never forget!"

You know it! Becky thought. *Let's hope it's the last one here, too! The very last dinner!*

CHAPTER 4

It was a warm July morning, with the sun already streaming through the light clouds. Just before eight-thirty, Becky pedaled her bike in front of Tricia's and Melanie's as they rode to their first Saturday morning car washing job. As usual, they all wore cut-offs since car washing was dirty work.

Tricia caught up with Becky, then pedaled hard to pass. "Here come Jess and Cara!"

Sure enough, Jess and Cara were riding up from the opposite direction. The Hutchinsons—their usual first Saturday morning regulars for car washing—lived about halfway between their groups of houses. The good news was that today the Hutchinsons' dirty cars—a tan Mercury and a white Honda—were already parked in the driveway by their pale yellow two-story house.

Jess and Cara rode into the driveway first, and Becky pedaled faster, catching up with Tricia as they turned into the Hutchinsons' driveway.

Jess was parking her bike, and she turned to Becky with curiosity. "What happened at dinner last night?"

"I just want to tell it once, and I know everyone's going to ask," Becky answered.

She parked her bike alongside theirs, then grabbed the bucket of rags from her bike's handlebar. Tricia and Melanie had asked about last night's dinner, too, but she'd put them off so she could tell all of them at once. One time was enough. The only trouble was *now* was that time.

"I don't know where to begin," she admitted. "Let me think about it a little more."

She uncoiled a garden hose by the driveway and started spraying off the white Honda. If only explaining were as easy as their car washing system: spray off car, sponge with soapy water, spray off car again, wipe dry, wash windows, then wipe the car again. Maybe that's how she'd tell it, start when they arrived at the Bradshaws' house for dinner—

"Come on, Beck," Tricia coaxed as they all set to work on the Honda. "We're dying to know. Not just because we're nosey, either, but because we care about you."

"Maybe it's both—nosiness and caring," Becky answered.

"Mostly caring," Cara replied, and Becky knew that was probably true.

She drew a deep breath, then unreeled the disastrous evening—from Mr. Bradshaw and Bullwinkle greeting them at the front door, to Gram starting to like the idea of the wedding . . . about Julius Squeezer, the snake, slithering on the dining room table, making Mom and Amanda scream . . . and about the great poppyseed grime scare.

Becky wobbled her head and rolled her eyes. "Quinn thought someone was trying to kill him."

Jess laughed. "I can't believe it!"

"I still can't, either," Becky admitted.

Everyone added their "I-can't-believe-its!" then began to laugh, too. Remembering the look on Quinn's face, Becky finally had to smile herself.

"Sounds like a dramatic dinner, all right," Tricia said, wiping down the Honda with a soapy sponge. "I would love to play Amanda's part about when the snake got loose. I would love it . . . l-o-v-e it!" She grinned, then threw her head back, and shrieked a loud and terrified, "Yiiiiiiii! Yiiiiiiiiii!!!"

"Yiiiiiiiiiiiii!" Jess echoed.

Cara started a milder "Yiiii—" and Melanie tried to, but instead she doubled over, laughing.

"Stop that, you wackos!" Becky yelled as their laughter became wilder and wilder. "Stop it!"

Glancing at the house, she warned, "Look, there's Mrs. Hutchinson at the kitchen window! We'll lose this job if we're out here screaming like weirdos!"

She gave Mrs. Hutchinson an all's-fine wave, then got busy polishing the driver's outside mirror. "Anyhow, I wouldn't want to replay any of last night!"

Finally Tricia simmered down. "Are all the Bradshaw boys like that . . . you know, mischievous . . . or maybe I should say 'difficult'?"

"Jonathan and Charlie seem all right," Becky decided. "But I don't really know them, either. Besides, they leave for college next month, so maybe they don't care as much. Quinn's the one who *really* doesn't like us. He'll be a senior in high school. I don't know . . . he's not just mischievous or difficult. He seems angry . . . angry as can be deep inside."

"They sound interesting, anyhow," Jess put in.

"Interesting," Becky agreed, "but definitely not funny. It's not nearly so interesting when you're the one pushed into being a family."

"Blended, not pushed," Tricia corrected. "There's a big difference."

Pushed, Becky thought, too shocked by her best friend to argue. First Gram came around to favor the wedding—and now Tricia was talking about being in a "blended family" as if it were no big deal. *Doesn't anyone understand how I feel?*

Cara was rinsing the soapy water from the Honda's trunk. "Let me tell you, it's not easy to be *blended* into a family," she put in, probably because she had a half sister. "But Bear told me that even having regular brothers and sisters can be a mixed bag. It's not like choosing your own friends."

Bear was the youth pastor at Santa Rosita Community Church, where they all went, even Jess and Cara lately. "Bear told you that?" Becky asked. "That having real brothers and sisters can be a mixed bag?"

Cara nodded. "He thinks that God gives us some . . . you know . . . difficult people in our lives to make us stronger . . . especially for when we get married. He thinks it helps us to know how to make a better family ourselves someday."

"Who needs it?" Becky complained, scrubbing the car harder. "Anyhow, I am not getting married yet! Probably not for ages."

"We'll all help you as much as we can," Melanie promised. "In this club we should all help each other."

"Right!" Tricia agreed. "We've always helped each other, even if it is a working club."

"I think my brothers know Quinn Bradshaw from high school," Jess said. "Maybe they can 'get something' on him."

"Thanks," Becky said. Not that 'getting something' on Quinn would do much good. The real question was: What could they do to stop the wedding?

Suddenly a brainstorm hit.

Maybe at Mrs. L.'s engagement party her friends could do something wild to stop it. . . .

Jess was scrubbing the tires hard. "Tell us about the Bradshaws' house," she said, maybe because her mom was a realtor.

At least that was easier to tell, but not funny, either. "What do you want to know?"

"For example," Cara said, "will you have your own room?"

"Yeah," Becky answered. "Except it's Quinn's room now. You should see it. There's a greasy carburetor on his desk—"

"A carburetor!" Tricia echoed with disbelief.

"The carburetor for his car," Becky explained. "A *greasy* carburetor. Also, there's a fish tank with a hot rock in it for Julius, the python. And one of those toddler gates at his door, with wire screening on it so Julius Squeezer can't escape into the rest of the house."

"Ufff!" Melanie uttered as she wiped the car's front window. "And I thought my brother William was bad, dressing up those lizards with foil!" She glanced at Becky with sympathy. "Where's Quinn going to move to?"

"Next to the garage, in his mother's potting shed."

"You're kidding!" Tricia replied.

"You'll have to forgive a former New Yorker," Melanie said, "but what exactly is a potting shed?"

"Most people here in Santa Rosita Estates don't have them, either," Becky told her. She tried to think how to explain. "You know, it's like a studio attached to the garage, where you keep vases, flower pots, leftover dried flowers, and other planting stuff. His mother, who died, used to make wreaths there, and other craft things for selling."

"Sounds cold in the winter," Jess said.

"No, it has heat . . . even a high-beamed wooden ceiling, tiled floor, and some beat-up antique furniture," Becky said. "It's a little rustic, but okay. He actually *wants* to move there. Probably to be with Julius, the python. Quinn could have the guest bedroom in the house if he wanted. There are five bedrooms upstairs."

Last night, after dinner, they'd inspected the house from top to bottom. Upstairs, there was a huge bedroom for Mom and Mr. Bradshaw, smaller bedrooms for Amanda and her, a big room to be shared by Jonathan and Charlie, who would return to college soon, and the nice guest bedroom.

Becky felt a flush of embarrassment, remembering what had happened. When Gram had asked how everyone wanted things decorated, Becky had blurted, "I like my old room that I have now!"

"Then we'll copy it exactly," Gram had promised.

But it won't be the same, Becky thought then, and she thought it again now. *No matter how exactly it's copied, it will never be my same room.*

Maybe she should have told her family what she'd been thinking, she thought as she polished the Honda.

"Come on, let's wash the Mercury," Tricia suggested. "This car's done. Look at it sparkle!"

Done. That's exactly how I feel, Becky thought. As if the very best part of her life were entirely d-o-n-e.

When Becky came home at one o'clock, Mom was sitting

halfway in the kitchen and halfway in the small utility room, ironing clothes. Cradling the phone against one ear, she gave Becky a smile, then said into the mouthpiece, "It sounds like a wonderful idea, Paul."

Becky's brain went on alert, and her body stiffened. *What's a wonderful idea?*

Determined to listen, she quietly got out the bread and dill pickles from the refrigerator, then the jar of peanut butter from a nearby cabinet. Who knew what Mom and Mr. Bradshaw might be dreaming up next?

"No problem," Mom was saying to him. "It's a good week for me to take a few days off."

Becky slathered the peanut butter on the bread. Time off? Mom was taking days off from work? That was different!

"Good," Mom told him. She turned her head away to be more private. "Ummmmm . . . oh, Paul. . . !"

Disgusting! Becky thought. How could Mom betray Dad like this? Where was her loyalty? Hadn't she ever loved Dad?

"Becky just came home," Mom told him in a normal voice. "I'll make certain she doesn't have any other plans. Fine. We'll leave tomorrow afternoon."

Tomorrow afternoon?! Becky's mind echoed. *What are they planning now?*

She smacked her pickle and peanut butter sandwich together, put it on a paper plate, and stuck it all in the microwave to cook for twenty seconds. When the microwave beeped, she was glad to hear that Mom was hanging up.

"Well, Beck," Mom said, "I have exciting news for you."

"What's that?" Becky asked warily.

Mom grinned from over the ironing board, where she was pressing one of her work blouses. "A new adventure for us.

We're going on a camping trip with the Bradshaws tomorrow. We'll be camping in the mountains for three days."

"Camping?!" Becky repeated, not quite believing it. Her family had never gone camping.

"Yep, camping," Mom answered. "They go every year for a week in August. Paul and I thought that . . . well, after last night, it would be a good idea for all of us to get to know each other better. They've invited us to go along, but we're cutting it down to three days because of the wedding. We leave Sunday after church and come home Wednesday night. Gram's going, too."

"Gram's going camping?"

"Yes, Gram. Remember, she used to camp a lot when she was a girl?"

Becky faintly recalled hearing Gram tell about it. "How are we all going to fit in one car?"

"Paul is driving us," Mom said, "and the boys are driving up together."

It sounded all decided, no matter what, Becky thought. "What do his boys . . . his sons . . . think about us going?"

"They're probably discussing it now," Mom said. "I'm sure they'll think it's a good idea, too."

Becky felt doubtful.

Suddenly she had an awful thought. "What about my slumber party tomorrow night?"

"Oh no!" Mom let out a remorseful breath. "I'm sorry, Beck. There's so much going on, I just plain forgot. You could postpone the slumber party. Have it next weekend."

"But everyone's planning to come—"

"I'm sorry, Beck," Mom apologized. "I'm really sorry, but I think it's for the best in the long run for all of us. You'll just have to call everyone and tell them you have to postpone the slumber party a week."

"What about my being president of the Twelve Candles Club? Doesn't *that* count?"

Mom's blue-green eyes met hers with regret. "That's why you have a vice-president. I'm sure Jess can run the club for three days. You have a long time to be president."

Tears flooded Becky's eyes. "But I don't want to go, Mom! I don't want to go camping!"

"But I think you should," her mother said firmly. "You can cry if you want to, but it won't change things. I can understand your reluctance, but no matter how you feel, I'm marrying Paul Bradshaw. It's not just a matter of my wanting to . . . which I truly do . . . but it's for the long-term good of both of our families."

Anger dried Becky's tears. It was clear there was no sense in arguing now. Instead, she spouted a resentful, "All right, I'll give up all of my jobs! I have to miss Morning Fun for Kids on Monday and Wednesday . . . and a clowning birthday party Monday afternoon. . . and two baby-sitting jobs."

"Thank you, Becky," Mom said, unflinching. "I'm glad to see that you're becoming so mature."

I'm not becoming mature about this! Becky thought, burning inside. *And I don't want to be, either!*

She tried to think up more excuses to stop the camping trip, but Mom was already folding up the ironing board with such determination, it looked as if she'd folded up all possible arguments with it.

Once Mom left the kitchen, Becky grabbed the phone. She'd have to do it, that's all. Best to start with Jess. She'd just tell her they were going out of town. A good thing the club had fewer jobs this week than last, and that Melanie had been accepted as a new member.

Jess answered her phone on the first ring. Once she understood the problem, she said, "Hey, I'm really sorry, Beck. Remember I told you I'd have the meetings and the club could use my phone, but nothing else? I'm too busy with gymnastics. I really am."

"But I won't be here," Becky said. "What could we do?"

"Search me," Jess answered, "you're the president. Besides, my family's going to Catalina Island for a few days."

"Maybe . . . maybe Melanie could be the back-up person for all of us. Sort of a general assistant."

"Sounds good if she'll do it," Jess said. She paused, then asked, "Where are you going anyhow?"

"Our family is going camping in the mountains with the Bradshaw family," Becky explained with reluctance. "You know, so we can get to know each other better before the wedding."

"Camping!" Jess said. "I didn't know your family ever camped."

"We don't. And would you believe even Gram is going?"

"You'll have fun," Jess assured her. "It'll be a first. By the way, does your mother have an engagement ring yet?"

"No . . . no, she doesn't." Everything had happened so quickly, an engagement ring hadn't even occurred to her. "No, not yet."

"Then maybe they're not really as serious as it sounds," Jess suggested.

Maybe not! Becky hoped. *Maybe not!!!!!!!*

"Give your jobs to Cara," Jess said in her usual take-charge manner. "She needs the money most."

"Are you suggesting or telling?"

Jess gave a laugh. "A little of each, I guess."

After they'd hung up, Becky called Tricia, who already knew the news. "Mom has me getting out our sleeping bags and stuff for you to borrow. You'll love camping! I promise, you'll love it!"

"Tricia! I thought you were my best friend."

"I am, old friendo. Listen, I think you may as well enjoy the camping trip, no matter what happens. You might never have another chance to go camping."

"Fine friend you are!" Becky said. As it was, she was still smarting over Tricia's remark this morning about becoming a *blended* family.

It took nearly half an hour of phone calls to rearrange her life, and Melanie was more than willing to be a general assistant when someone couldn't come to meetings. "I am honored" was exactly what she'd said.

Finally, Becky called her baby-sitting clients, and they agreed to having Cara work for them instead.

After that, she had eight pizza party invitations to make for Morelli's Pizza Parlor. She was still gluing the dried pepperoni slices on the poster board cards when Mom and Mr. Bradshaw left for their dinner and movie date.

Through it all, though, the thought that lingered in Becky's mind was what Jess had expressed: *Maybe they're really not serious since Mom doesn't have an engagement ring.*

Maybe this camping trip would stop the wedding.

Maybe somehow it'd bring Mom and Mr. Bradshaw's romance to an absolute end.

CHAPTER

5

At Sunday breakfast, Mom helped herself to a waffle, then smiled at Becky and Amanda. "Let's ride to church together."

"I usually ride with Tricia and my other TCC friends," Becky objected, even though it seemed she was forever objecting lately. But she had a good reason. Her whole life was being turned upside down.

"Me too!" Amanda joined in from across the breakfast table. "We have lots of fun in Mrs. Bennett's minivan. I like to ride with them."

"You just like to be with Bryan," Becky said, since Amanda considered Bryan Bennett her boyfriend.

Amanda raised her chin, then made a fake smiley-face. "Maybe I do, and maybe I don't."

"Back to the subject," Mom said firmly. "I'd like for all of us to ride together this morning."

Becky drew a deep breath. "If you say so."

"I say so," Mom answered lightly. "In fact, I told the Bennetts that you'd be riding with me this morning when I borrowed their camping equipment."

It was scary to think what other plans Mom and Mr. Bradshaw might have made on their date last night. There hadn't been much time yesterday to even discuss the camping trip. Mom had run out shopping twice between the times she'd supervised their packing, and she'd had a million phone calls. Between that, she'd somehow baked a chocolate chip cake, cranberry-nut muffins, peanut butter cookies, and candied pecans, making the house smell wonderful again for a change.

She wants to impress the Bradshaw boys with goodies, Becky thought. In fact, when she'd asked to try a cookie, Mom had said, "It's all for the camping trip. So are the soft drinks in the fridge. It's the least we can do. Paul is bringing steaks and hamburgers and so much else."

Mom glanced at her wristwatch. "Come on, we'd better hurry or we'll be late for church. Thank goodness we're packed for the trip. We'll just have some fast sandwiches here for lunch before the Bradshaws pick us up."

Amanda finished chewing some waffle. "Is Quinn taking his snake along?"

"No way!" Mom exclaimed.

Too bad, Becky thought. The snake was a remote—very remote—possibility to keep Mom from marrying Mr. Bradshaw.

"Are they taking Bullwinkled?" Amanda asked.

"Bullwinkle," Mom corrected. "And I doubt that they'll take him because there are bears in the mountains."

"Bears?" Becky repeated. "I'm not camping with bears!"

"They won't be near us," Mom assured her. "Eat faster

now. Not so much talking . . . we need to get going."

But Becky no longer felt hungry, and the waffle was hard to swallow. Even her peeled orange smelled sour. It was bad enough to give up her TCC jobs; now she had to go camping—and not only with the Bradshaw family, but with bears!

Later, in the garage, when they climbed into Mom's green Oldsmobile, Becky let Amanda sit in the front seat without squabbling about it.

"Why don't you want to sit here?" her sister asked.

Becky slammed her back car door shut. "I'd just like to sit here alone and think."

Mom was locking the inside garage door that led into the kitchen. *Probably worried someone will steal the muffins, cake, and cookies!* Becky thought.

Amanda turned to the backseat. "Are you mad at Mom?"

Becky considered the question. "I guess I'm mostly mad at . . . at . . . circumstances."

"Who's that?" Amanda asked.

"Never mind!" Becky shot back, since Mom was opening her car door. No sense in bringing up the worst thing of all: If Dad hadn't died, this wouldn't be happening!

As they backed the car out of the garage, Becky saw the Bennetts' van was already a block down the street. The big romance was not only ruining their family, but cutting into her friendships. And even into the Club.

As they drove down their street, Mom said, "Paul and I made some decisions last night. Becky, we'd like you to be my maid of honor at the wedding. You know, like a bridesmaid."

"What?!" Becky asked.

Mom didn't stop. "That means you'd walk up the aisle before me, then later, hand me Paul's ring and take my bouquet of flowers. And, Amanda, we'd like you to be our flower girl."

Becky sat stunned. *Me, your maid of honor?!*

Amanda was asking a million questions. Finally she asked, "You mean I throw flowers on the church aisle in front of you?"

Mom laughed. "That's exactly the job of a flower girl. We'll have a special white runner up the middle aisle, and that's where you'll throw them."

She flipped on the turn signal for Ocean Avenue, and it clicked loudly in the car. "Gram wants to buy both of you bridal party dresses for the wedding."

"Wedding dresses?!" Becky asked to be sure.

"Yes, you might call them that. We thought a pale blue for you, Becky . . . and maybe a pale yellow for you, Amanda."

Amanda sang out, "I l-o-v-e yellow! I love yellow!"

Becky felt so dazed, she could only ask, "Gram wants to buy the wedding dresses?"

"Yes, you know her generous heart," she answered. Once Amanda had quieted, Mom asked, "Well . . . how would you like to be my maid of honor, Beck?"

"I—I'd like to think about it."

"Fine," Mom said. "One other thing, we're having a reception in the church lounge after the wedding. We'll have punch and hors d'oeuvres, and wedding cake for dessert. I thought the Twelve Candles Club might be interested in helping for two hours. Not you, of course, but the other girls."

"They're already helping for Mrs. Llewellyn's engagement party Friday night!" Becky protested.

"The wedding's a week later, on the Saturday after that," Mom pointed out.

No way can they help! Becky thought. *No way!*

"You don't have to help, of course," Mom said. "I just

thought it'd be nice to have all of the girls there. It's an important time in your life, too. Besides, it might look bad if we hired someone else."

"Maybe the Twelve Candles girls would think you don't like 'em!" Amanda said, wide-eyed at the thought.

Becky asked her mother, "Is that Mrs. Wurtzel going to do the catering?"

Mom shook her head, her eyes watching traffic. "No, some of the ladies from church. They'd be willing to serve, too, if you don't want your friends there."

Becky remembered Amanda's warning: *The Twelve Candles girls would think you don't like 'em.*

Finally she decided. "We may as well ask them, since they're working for the engagement party anyhow."

Mom stopped their car for the red light before they turned off Ocean Avenue. "I'm glad you want them there. Our lives are going to be very different after the wedding, you know."

"What else?!" Becky asked in alarm.

Mom glanced at her in the rearview mirror. "I'm going to stop working."

"You're going to stop working?!" Becky exclaimed. It was such a surprise, especially since Mom had just gotten a wonderful job that paid lots of money.

"Marrying Paul has given me that option . . . and I would really prefer to be at home with you girls," Mom answered. "There's so many more family things we could do, and the truth is, I'm not all that happy working in an office. I've been an at-home mom, and now I've tried having a really good job for a career. I like the at-home career best of all."

Is that why you're marrying Mr. Bradshaw?! So you won't have to work?

Mom's eyes met hers in the rearview mirror, and it was as if she'd read Becky's mind again. "No, Beck, that's not why I'm marrying Paul Bradshaw. The truth is that, little by little, I've fallen in love with him."

"But what about Dad?" Becky finally blurted. "I thought you loved Dad!"

"This is different," Mom answered calmly. "I still love your father, and I'll never forget him. But I believe that God has sent a new husband and father into our lives."

"I can't believe it!" Becky exclaimed.

"I didn't at first, either," Mom said, "but I do now. And I feel certain that your father would approve of my marrying Paul Bradshaw. He would have really liked him."

Becky just barely kept the tears back. *I'll never believe it! I'll never in all of my life believe it! Only one good thing has happened since Dad died—Mom and I got closer . . . that is, until now. She talked things over with me as if I were a grown-up, and she used to ask me for my opinion before making decisions. Now she's just telling me what she and that Paul guy have already decided, and I don't have any say in the matter. She doesn't need me at all anymore, 'cause she's got Paul Bradshaw.*

Now I don't even have a dad or a mom!

At Sunday school, Becky could scarcely sing or concentrate on what Bear, the youth pastor, was saying.

"What's with you, Beck?" Tricia whispered from beside her. "You seem a million miles away."

Becky just shook her head and tuned back into the Sunday school class. Bear was saying, "Jesus is the light of the world. No matter how your life is going, He wants us near Him—so we can lighten up the world around us! Do you hear me, folks? Lighten up!"

Later, standing in front of the church entrance after the service, Mom and Paul Bradshaw held hands as they told their church friends the big news.

Urk. Becky gulped and tried to look away.

Jonathan, Charlie, and Quinn Bradshaw had come with their father, and even they eyed the hand-holding uneasily.

Gram came by, and one of her much older friends asked Mom, "Do you have an engagement ring yet?"

Mom and Mr. Bradshaw just shook their heads and laughed.

Becky didn't see anything funny about it. No engagement ring was a good sign since for sure Mr. Bradshaw could afford one. Yes, it only made sense. If they were really going to get married, he'd give Mom an engagement ring. . . .

Driving home from church, Amanda and Mom talked on and on about the wedding. And, in the backseat, Becky prayed, "Lord, please don't let there ever be an engagement ring! And no matter what, please don't let there be a wedding!"

At home, they changed for the camping trip. Both Mom and Becky wore jeans and white Tees; the difference was Mom looked beautiful in her snug-fitting jeans and softly curved Tee. She wore her hair pulled back in a ponytail, like a girl. "Why don't you wear your cowgirl boots?" Mom suggested to Becky.

"No way!" Becky objected. "I'm not going to have everyone laughing at me. It's not like working at Mrs. Llewellyn's western party, when we were supposed to."

Mom smiled. "It's up to you."

We might be going camping, Becky thought, *but that doesn't mean I have to look like a cowgirl.* Anyhow, she was wearing her new white visor with the big blue glass jewels on the front. It'd been a reassuring sight in the mirror, making her look more grown-up. Besides, the blue jewels matched her eyes.

Mom smiled right through lunch, as if she had a wonderful secret. When they finished eating, she said, "Pile up your duffle and sleeping bags by the front door. Gram's bringing her cooler for our drinks and baked goods. And Paul should be here any moment."

Amanda hopped up from the table and twirled into the living room. "Camping . . . camping! We're going camping! Camping . . . camping. . . !"

Mom laughed. "Oh, Amanda, you're a love . . . and a character! Don't forget to bring your things to the door."

Amanda flew off to her room, and Becky noticed that Mom didn't say *she* was "a love" or "a character."

While she trudged toward her room, her sister zoomed out carrying her borrowed duffle and the sleeping bags. As usual, Buster Bunny was jammed under her arm. "We're going camping!" she sang out, ignoring Becky's cross look.

Finally, Becky made her way through the living room with the sleeping and duffle bags Mom had borrowed for her from Tricia. The sleeping bag had a peculiar lump in it, but now was no time for examining it. Besides, Amanda still danced about wildly, and despite everything, Becky felt just a little excited herself.

They'd no more than dumped everything by the door when Mr. Bradshaw arrived, backing an old tan van into the driveway.

"Where's his dark blue Cadillac?" Becky asked.

"It's not much good for camping," Mom answered. She eyed herself in the mirror and fussed with her hair. "He's had the van for years, mostly for camping."

Well, what do you know? Becky thought as she opened the front door.

As he climbed from the driver's seat, Mr. Bradshaw grinned from ear to ear above his short beard. He wore jeans and old boots, looking entirely different . . . almost like a cowboy.

"Hi, Becky . . . Amanda . . . Libby," he called out. "Is everyone ready?"

"We're ready," Mom said, "except Gram isn't here yet." She gave a laugh. "You've got yourself quite a family."

"I know," he said to Mom. They looked at each other as if they shared secrets, then as if they wanted to kiss!

Uffff!!! Becky grabbed her duffle and sleeping bags and carried them to his van. *D-i-s-g-u-s-t-i-n-g!*

Gram drove up in her new white Oldsmobile singing, "I'm an old cowhand. . . ." Usually she wore dresses or suits, but now she wore old jeans, a blue shirt, a red bandana around her neck—and cowgirl boots. Not only that, she was acting like she was young.

Gram saw Becky staring at her and laughed. "I knew if I hung on to this outfit long enough, it would come in handy. What do you think, Beck?"

It flashed through Becky's mind that maybe Mr. Bradshaw would want to marry Gram instead of Mom, and that wouldn't be so bad. "It's all right, if you want to look like a cowgirl."

"Just the look I was after," Gram admitted with a laugh. She reached into her car for her video camera, then grabbed a bag from the seat. "I bought red bandanas for everybody as a memento of this occasion. One for each of us. I bought some for Jonathan, Charlie, and Quinn, too. And we can't forget the cooler in the trunk. I made beans, coleslaw, and my best potato salad, not to mention carrot and celery sticks."

"You're going to spoil us," Mr. Bradshaw said as he and Mom stepped outside.

They accepted their red bandanas from Gram and happily began to tie them around their necks. When they'd finished, Mom adjusted Mr. Bradshaw's bandana, and they stood admiring each other.

"Let's go," Becky suggested. "Let's go!"

"Glad to see you're so eager, Becky," Mr. Bradshaw remarked with a chuckle. "I didn't know you'd feel so excited about camping."

"She's going to love it, pardner," Gram declared. "She'll be happier than an old coyote with a full moon."

I don't think so, Becky was thinking. *I don't think so!*

Mom said, "Becky, be sure to bring a sketching pad."

"Maybe I will," Becky said. "I'll get it now." She ran to her room, mostly to escape them.

Hours later, they arrived in the forested mountains. The van wound around one hillside after another, making the camping equipment roll and bang around behind them in the van. Mom and Mr. Bradshaw sat in the front seat, and Gram sat between Amanda and Becky in the middle seat, Gram teaching Amanda crazy camping songs.

At long last, Mr. Bradshaw slowed the van. "There are the campgrounds. Up this road, back in the forest."

"Thank goodness," Becky grumbled.

"Haven't you enjoyed this?" Gram asked.

"Not so far," Becky admitted, then turned toward the window.

"You're changing, Beck," Gram said, frowning a bit. "I do believe you're changing."

"Me?" Becky asked. "*I'm* changing?"

"Yes," Gram answered. "You've always been so bright and cheery."

Suddenly Bear's words returned to Becky. *Jesus wants us near Him, so that we can lighten up. Do you hear me, folks? Lighten up!*

CHAPTER

6

As Mr. Bradshaw parked the van in their campground space, Becky glanced at their surroundings. The forest hid tents, campers, and vans, making the campground seem less crowded; and the smell of campfires filled the mountain air. Not far away stood redwood picnic tables, also a stone barbecue with firewood and a big cook grill. It was probably all right for camping, Becky thought.

Behind her, Amanda climbed out of the van, asking Mr. Bradshaw, "Where's your boys?"

"They'll be coming along later," he replied. "Why? Do you miss them, Amanda?"

She scrunched up her face and shook her head no, making him laugh.

Then Mom said, "Why, Amanda Hamilton, I'm surprised at you. That isn't at all polite!"

Becky silently agreed with her sister. Thank goodness his

"boys" weren't already here at the campground.

Mr. Bradshaw gave a nod toward the next camping space. "They'll be pitching another tent right there. A good thing we reserved two adjacent spaces."

He smiled at Mom. "And that was before I knew you last year. I must admit, though, I was noticing you at church."

Mom teased, "Oh, you did, did you?"

A good thing they had two spaces, all right, Becky decided. One for the "women's tent" on this space, and the neighboring space for the "men's tent," as Mom and Mr. Bradshaw called them. As far as Becky was concerned, ten million miles apart would be far better. As it was, only a tall pine tree and grass separated their dusty camping spaces.

"Let's set up your tent now," Mr. Bradshaw said. He opened the van's back door and wrestled the green canvas tent out. "How good of the Bennetts to lend us their camping gear."

"It was, wasn't it?" Mom said. "We didn't have a thing." She grabbed an end of the tent. "I'm afraid I won't be much help. I don't have any idea how to set up a tent."

Gram helped with carrying the tent, too. "Stand back, Libby girl," she said, "Paul and I will show you how."

"She may even decorate it for us," Mom laughed.

Gram grinned. "At least it looks like an old-fashioned tent, the kind I know how to put up. That's right, you said it had belonged to Tricia's grandparents."

Sure enough, it didn't take long to set the tent in place. Mr. Bradshaw began to pound in the tent stakes, and Gram hurried over to the van to get her video camera. Mom headed for the tent flap, Becky and Amanda right behind her.

"Maybe you'd better wait till I've pounded all the stakes in," Mr. Bradshaw suggested.

"We'll be careful," Mom promised.

"Just so you don't bump the tent now," he warned.

"Why, Paul Bradshaw," Mom teased, "do we look as if we're tent bumpers?"

He laughed. "I'm not so sure."

Mom told Becky and Amanda, "We can at least put down the ground cloth and bring our sleeping and duffle bags in."

They headed for the back of the van.

Gram zoomed in on them with her video camera as Mom took out the ground cloth, and Becky tugged out "her" sleeping bag. Becky noticed the suspicious bump in the bag again and gave it a squeeze. Whatever it might be, it was hard—nothing she wanted to sleep on. What on earth had Tricia left in there?

Putting the ground cloth down in the tent with Mom and Amanda was fairly easy. That finished, Becky grabbed her sleeping bag.

"Look," she told Amanda, "there's something in Tricia's sleeping bag."

Amanda eyed it warily. "Maybe a snake!"

"Yipes! No, it's too hard," Becky answered, not too worried. After all, Mom was in the tent with them, and Mr. Bradshaw was right outside, pounding in stakes.

Amanda still eyed the lump uneasily, but Becky unrolled the bag with a show of courage.

Suddenly a bug-eyed green animal leapt out at her.

"Yiiii!" she screamed as it rushed at her and bounced off her chest. "Yiiiiiii!"

Amanda shrieked just as loudly, and next to them, Mom screamed, "Paul!!!!"

Together, they jumped away against the tent, tilting up its

other side. They squealed even more loudly as the folds of canvas buckled, swooshed, and collapsed heavily, knocking them onto their backs on the ground.

Outside, Paul had yelled, "What on earth. . . ?"

"They're in it!" Gram yelled. "They're in the tent!"

"Help!" Becky shouted, struggling with the folds of canvas around her. "Help! We're all tangled up . . . and there's a big green a-n-i-m-a-l in here!!!!!"

"Animal?!!!" Mr. Bradshaw repeated.

Amanda wailed beside Becky, and behind them Mom was calling out, "Pull it back off of us!" then, "Quiet, Amanda!"

Despite the mess, it occurred to Becky that this might be the very thing to stop the wedding! Maybe Mom would hate camping and get mad at him—

"Everyone stay calm!" Mr. Bradshaw told them, not sounding too calm himself. "We'll have you out of there in short order. You all right in there?"

"So far!" Mom gasped. "I'm trying to lift the canvas off us. Girls, help!"

As they struggled with the heavy green canvas, Becky heard more concerned voices shouting.

Somehow Mom and Becky raised the canvas enough to make a cavelike opening in the green darkness. Luckily, there was no sign of the animal, and they were all fine.

All of a sudden, Mom began to laugh while their rescuers worked around them, pulling and yanking the tent off of them.

"What's so funny?" Becky asked. "We could suffocate in here!"

"I doubt it," Mom gasped. "What's so funny is our overpowering predicament!"

Before long, the tent was pulled upright again.

"Whew!" Becky exclaimed. In the dust beside her, she noticed her white visor with the blue glass jewels and stuck it back on her head. At least it wasn't lost.

As they rose to their feet, they saw the new rescuers—Charlie, Jonathan, and Quinn. What's more, the three of them began to laugh, quietly at first, then harder and harder! People camping all around got in the spirit and gathered around to join in the hilarity.

"It was . . . worth coming," Charlie gasped, ". . . just to see that!"

Blood rushed to Becky's cheeks.

E-m-b-a-r-r-a-s-s-i-n-g!

In the midst of the laughter, Becky's eyes lit on the green animal, which was bigger than a huge fist. "There it is! That big frog by the tent flap! There was nothing funny about it jumping right out of Tricia's sleeping bag at us!"

Charlie picked it up gingerly, and then began to laugh again. "It's plastic . . . and spring-loaded. It even has a note taped to it."

Becky grabbed the frog from him. "Guess it's supposed to be for me."

The note, she saw, was signed: "Tricia, also known as El Froggo." Becky quickly tore it off the frog and crumpled the paper up fiercely. The message had said, "Lighten up!"

Stung with hurt, Becky went over to the van and sat down on the back bumper away from everybody. *They're all one big happy family, and they're all laughing at me. They don't care about my feelings. They're too busy having their own fun. Well, who needs them? And I don't need Tricia's little sermons!*

Finally, when the others had enough laughing, Mr. Bradshaw suggested, "Come on, fellows, let's finish this one, then get the 'men's tent' up. This time, no one goes inside till all the stakes are knocked in."

Mom gave a laugh again. "I told you we're inexperienced."

" 'Inexperienced' is the word for it!" he laughed. "And I can't think when I've enjoyed inexperienced campers more. After I saw all of you were safe, of course."

"Of course!" Mom teased, and everyone laughed again.

Uffffff, Becky thought. Getting up, she walked to the tent and stuck El Froggo back into her sleeping bag. If Tricia weren't her best friend, she would gladly wring her neck.

"If only we had a picture of the entire episode," Mr. Bradshaw said.

Gram stepped up with her video camera. "I do believe I got all of it on video."

"You didn't!" Mom laughed.

"I did," Gram admitted, grinning. "For a change, I wasn't at all worried about your survival. The scene is filmed for posterity."

Everyone chuckled, and this time Becky had to smile herself. Surprisingly, smiling felt good. Maybe she'd do just what Bear—and now Tricia—said: try to lighten up. But it didn't mean she was giving in to Mom and Paul. She'd still watch for every possible way to s-t-o-p t-h-e w-e-d-d-i-n-g.

An hour later, the tents were up, and the smell of hamburgers and corn-on-the-cob filled the campground. The men pushed two redwood picnic tables together. Then Becky and Amanda wiped them off and covered them with Gram's red and white checkered plastic tablecloths. Next, they helped Mom and Gram put out the dip, chips, pickles, coleslaw, potato salad, and carrot and celery sticks. And last, they set out peanut butter cookies and the large pan of chocolate chip cake. Jonathan Bradshaw beamed. "Just look at that!"

"Doesn't it look good?" Charlie added, licking his lips. He turned to Mom and Gram. "You're going to spoil us."

Mom laughed. "I hope so! I hope to spoil you so badly that you can't wait to come home from college."

Quinn's eyes lit up at the sight of the food, but he turned away quickly.

Just like she felt, Becky thought. Even though the food smelled and looked good, feeding the Bradshaws so well was not apt to turn them against the wedding. Becky glanced at the nearby forest rising higher and higher into the mountains. Maybe bears would come out to eat up the dinner. . . .

Finally, the corn and hamburgers were ready, and everyone sat down at the long table, passing around the pickles, ketchup, mustard, and sliced tomatoes.

"Let's join hands and give thanks," Mr. Bradshaw said.

Sitting between Gram and Amanda, Becky was glad she wouldn't have to hold Bradshaw hands. It was bad enough to be sitting across from Quinn, who glowered at her. Luckily if she kept her head down, her white visor hid him from view.

"Dear Heavenly Father," Mr. Bradshaw began, "we come to you with grateful hearts for this beautiful forest and the mountains that surround us . . . we thank you for the loving family all around us, and for this food. . . ."

Becky's mind stopped on the words "loving family." He meant all of them. Well, she sure didn't want to be part of it! His other words fell away from her until the "Amen."

As she bit into her juicy hamburger, Quinn muttered loud enough so she could hear, "Looks like frog meat to me."

She glared at him, though it didn't faze him. Everybody was laughing at her, even sour old Quinn. No, she was *not* going to be "blended" into this family.

That night, a ranger program was held by a big campfire. They sat on rows of benches and sang lots of old songs, and the coyotes seemed to be howling off and on far in the hills.

When they returned to the tents with their flashlights, someone said they'd heard of bears nearby. Worst of all, they had to find their way from their tent to the camp's cement block building with restrooms and showers. Becky carried a flashlight, and so did the others, but the scary shadows around the trees loomed in the darkness.

How would she ever be able to sleep here? she wondered as she stumbled back into the tent. She perched El Froggo on top of her nearby duffle bag as if he were their watch-frog against bears, coyotes, and other varmints. She'd no more than settled herself in Tricia's sleeping bag when her worries floated off into the darkness and she fell asleep.

The next morning, the aromas of coffee and frying bacon awakened her. Becky rolled over in her sleeping bag, but Amanda was already awake. "Camping's fun, isn't it, Becky?" she asked.

Becky closed her eyes, unwilling to admit that camping had its good moments, such as singing at the campfire last night.

"Mom's already up," Amanda informed her. "She's helping Mr. Bradshaw get breakfast. They really like each other!"

"Maybe he'll like Gram better," Becky answered.

"No way!" Amanda exclaimed.

Becky didn't say anything, though she was pretty sure that

it wasn't Gram whom Mr. Bradshaw liked so much.

"You think it's the same way I like Bryan?" Amanda asked.

"I don't think so," Becky answered, dragging herself out of the sleeping bag. Glancing around inside the tent, she saw Gram was up, too. And there was El Froggo, the watch-frog, who really wasn't any help.

Becky pulled on her jeans and sweatshirt, then Amanda wanted help with her clothes. At long last, they were dressed, and Becky settled her jeweled visor on her hair and forehead. When they made their way through the tent flap, Mom, Gram, and Mr. Bradshaw greeted them with hearty "Good-mornings!"

"Morning," Becky managed. She cast a suspicious glance at Mom and Mr. Bradshaw, who sat eating breakfast at the picnic table. They looked more secretive than usual.

"I've taken over the cooking," Gram said, stationed by the grill. "What's your pleasure? We have bacon, scrambled eggs, pancakes, and your mom's delicious cranberry-nut muffins. There's also orange juice in those plastic containers on the table."

Becky felt hungry, really hungry. "Bacon, eggs, and two pancakes, I guess," she decided, wishing she didn't feel so starved. It'd be better if she just marched away in a huff.

"Me too," Amanda added, then sat down happily at the table across from Mom and Mr. Bradshaw.

Becky sat down, not facing them. From the corner of her eye, she saw him dart a glance at Mom's beautiful slim fingers. Her fingers were bare! She wasn't wearing any rings this morning—not even Dad's engagement and wedding rings! It seemed to be some kind of a signal. No, she must be imagining. Anyway, Mom wasn't wearing an engagement ring from Mr. Bradshaw, either.

Still sitting, Mom poured juice into plastic glasses for Becky and Amanda. "You two slept like bears."

"Does that mean we snored?" Amanda inquired earnestly.

Mom laughed. "Only like hibernating bears."

"Where's everyone else?" Becky asked.

"Gone fishing," Mom answered. "As soon as you two finish breakfast, we thought we could all go pay the fishermen a visit. Let's hope they're catching lunch. Becky, you might want to bring your sketching pad."

Becky wasn't sure that she wanted to, but at least it would be something to do.

Before long, Gram arrived with plates heaped with bacon, eggs, and pancakes. "Isn't this fun?" she said, enthusiastic. "I wish we'd have taken your mother camping when she was a girl, but Gramp didn't care for it at all. Never thought I'd ever have a chance to camp again."

After breakfast, Gram insisted on cleaning up, too, so the rest of them could get going on their hike. Mom, Mr. Bradshaw, Amanda, and Becky headed out of the camp along a forested trail, Becky with her sketching pad in hand.

Sunshine filtered through the trees and shimmered on the distant mountains, and the air smelled crisp. Even when they'd hiked a long way, the breeze held the scent of campfires. And Becky was beginning to think that camping wasn't so bad, after all.

They made their way through the still forest for a long time, and the trail began to wind steeply downhill. Coming around a bend, they saw Jonathan, Charlie, and Quinn fishing by a winding stream. Quinn was on the closest side of the water, and Jonathan and Charlie must have crossed the nearby stone bridge, since they sat on big boulders on the other side.

"Any luck?" their father asked them.

"Not yet," Jonathan answered. "Just a few nibbles."

"Think I'll stay here and try to sketch for a while," Becky said when Mom and Mr. Bradshaw decided to hike farther on the trail.

"I'm going with them," Amanda announced.

Thank goodness, Becky thought.

She sat down on a big, flat rock some distance behind Quinn, set the visor lower over her eyes to shield them from the sun, and began to sketch the stream, forest, and mountains. It wasn't easy, especially to make the mountains appear as far away as they were. It was even more difficult with the strong morning breeze whipping her sketchbook pages.

She'd been sketching and erasing for a while when suddenly Quinn's fishing rod whirred, and he jumped to his feet.

"You've got one!" Charlie called from across the stream.

Quinn pulled on the pole and carefully played the fish along, until suddenly it was out of the water, slapping and flapping against the dust and weeds around Becky's feet.

"Gross!" she yelled, jumping up from the rock. "You almost touched me with it!"

Quinn ignored her, letting the fish flop all around her even longer.

He was doing it on purpose, she decided as she backed away. Finally, he grabbed onto it, and threaded the fish onto a stringer tied to a rock in the stream.

Becky sat back down on the rock behind Quinn and watched as he put a big ugly brown worm on his hook. Then he quickly flicked the fishing rod back and cast his line toward the stream. The hook and line swung back toward her, and she screamed as it hooked her new visor. In a flash, it landed right in the middle of the stream!

"My visor!" she yelled. "You hooked it on purpose!"

He shot a disgusted look at her, then reeled the line in. Her visor had become tangled up with the worm, and Becky could see brown worm specks stuck on the blue jewels. When he had the soggy thing in hand, he took it off the hook, bowed, and threw the visor to her. It landed with a wet smack in her hands.

"You did it on purpose," he mimicked, "ruining my worm!"

"I did not!"

"Did too!" he answered.

She couldn't help yelling, "There's no way I'd want you as a brother!"

"Believe me, the feeling is mutual," he replied angrily. "We don't want you!"

From across the stream, Jonathan called out, "Speak for yourself, Quinn."

"What about Mom?" Quinn shot back at him. "You think we should forget she ever existed?"

"And what about my dad?!" Becky answered angrily, not hearing Jonathan's answer. She kicked dried mud pieces at the river.

A moment later, Gram came up the trail, waving as if she hadn't heard their anger.

Becky pulled bits of worm from her visor, stuck the wet visor back on her head, and slapped her sketchbook shut.

"Let's catch up with Mom and the others," she said to Gram. "I'd like to see other places, too. Besides, it's getting too windy here." And she didn't mean just Quinn. The wind was growing stronger and stronger.

"Suits me just fine," Gram said. "After eating so much, I need a good hike."

At noon, there were piles of grilled fish to eat with the leftovers. The wind gusted harder and harder, though, whirling dust and twigs all around the table and the campsite. Napkins went flying, and dirt flew, making streaks on their dishes.

Before they'd finished eating, a park ranger in his uniform came to their table. "We have a weather warning for stronger winds. We're not closing the campground since it's just a warning, but we're expecting high winds for the next two days."

Mom and Mr. Bradshaw eyed each other with concern.

The wind whipped the nearby trees wildly, swirling clouds of dust. Nearby, a family was taking down their flapping tent and packing up their camper. Others had put bandanas up around their faces to keep the flying dust out.

"See how their faces are covered?" Mr. Bradshaw said. "Let's all put on our bandanas. And hope that the wind will die down."

Before long, they all wore their red bandanas like masks on their faces. It hardly kept the grit from blowing into their eyes. Jonathan and Charlie pulled out their sunglasses, and soon everyone was wearing dark glasses and red bandana masks. Bandits, Becky thought, we look like bandits. She almost laughed at the sight. The Bradshaw and Hamilton gangs. So much for camping!

Nearby, the wind whipped a tree so hard that a big branch cracked and fell onto a couple's tent. Luckily no one was in it.

"That's it," the woman said. "I'm not camping in this wind."

Mr. Bradshaw glanced at the trees bending and swirling

above their own campsite. "Maybe we'd better break camp ourselves. Better to be safe than sorry."

Becky's heart leapt with gratefulness. She'd had enough of the Bradshaw Gang already.

Everyone began to pack up their things and take the tents down. Becky felt as though God had answered her prayers, sending a wind storm to stop the wedding. The camping trip had been blown apart. She rushed around happily, carrying duffle and sleeping bags to the van.

She felt certain Mom and Mr. Bradshaw had brought them together on this camping trip to blend their families. It hadn't worked . . . it hadn't! Becky thought. What's more, if they tried any other "blending" ideas, she'd enlist the help of the Twelve Candles Club to "stir things up."

As she raced through the dust toward the van, she saw something sparkling on Mom's finger—

No . . . oh no! A million times NO!

A diamond engagement ring!

CHAPTER

7

The next few days, Becky was so busy with Twelve Candles Club jobs and the afternoon meetings that sometimes she almost forgot what was happening to her family. Almost. The hardest times were when Mr. Bradshaw came over. Or when Mom raved over what a fine man he was—or flashed her diamond engagement ring.

When Becky slowed down long enough to sit at the dining area table to make pizza party invitations, all she could think of were "if-onlys"—if only the wedding date *wasn't* coming closer . . . and if only the kitchen counter *wasn't* covered with lists . . . and if only Mom *wasn't* forever rushing around shopping and making the endless wedding arrangements.

On top of that, Gram had become so excited about the wedding, it was as if she were getting married. When she noticed Becky's glumness, she'd said, "We'll have such a good time together while your mom and Paul are in Israel on their honeymoon. I'll have the decorating under control, so we can go to the beach some mornings and rent good family videos—"

"I'll be working," Becky reminded her. "The Twelve Candles Club is getting loads of jobs."

"Of course, dear," Gram said soothingly. "But you need to take some time for fun, too."

"I like working," Becky had answered. "Lots of the jobs are fun. Yesterday I helped take Jojo and Jimjim Davis to Ocean World." No sense in saying that working helped her to forget that Friday night was the engagement party at Mrs. Llewellyn's and then, next Saturday afternoon would be the worst of all—the wedding.

On Friday morning, she trudged next door to the Bennetts' for Morning Fun for Kids, with Amanda at her side. Tricia had wanted to do a Magic Carpet Ride about camping, and Becky didn't care to ever hear another word on the subject. Finally she'd said, "Okay, go ahead and do it."

Today, since she was in charge of arts and crafts, Becky was going to have the visiting kids—the Funners—draw and cut out camping pictures with tents and trees and mountains.

Amanda walked beside her across their front lawn. "I'd like to go camping again with Mr. Bradshaw's family," she said. "Wouldn't you?"

"No way," Becky answered. Maybe some moments had been good, but the engagement ring had ruined it all.

"Why don't you like camping?" Amanda asked. "I liked it, even if the wind made us come home early. Maybe we can go again with Mr. Bradshaw."

"I don't want to talk about it!"

"Were you afraid of El Froggo and the tent falling on us?"

"Never mind, Amanda! And please be good this morning."

Amanda gave her a sideways glance. "You weren't very good on the camping trip."

"Never mind!" Becky said again. What a trial it could be to have a five-year-old sister.

"Anyhow, I like it when we dress alike," Amanda continued, referring to their white shorts and Tees. "It makes me feel like we're almost twins."

Best to change the subject, Becky decided. "You mean twins like Jimjim and Jojo Davis?"

"No way!" Amanda answered. "Not 'dentical twins."

"Identical," Becky corrected, though she felt like saying a good and clear "Never mind!" again. On the other hand, it was useless to argue with Amanda, who was always so terribly determined.

Becky noticed the usual yellow poster on the Bennetts' breezeway gate. It read,

MORNING FUN FOR KIDS
PLEASE KNOCK ON GATE

She reached over the top of the gate to unlatch it. Morning Fun for Kids had really turned out well. On Monday, Wednesday, and Friday mornings, from nine o'clock to noon, they had the crazy daycare for ten to fifteen kids aged four to seven, whom they called the Funners.

As they started through the breezeway, Becky thought again about how ideal the Bennetts' fenced yard was for the Funners. It held a colorful gym set, swings, a sandbox, and a tree house in the overgrown pepper tree. The redwood picnic table and benches on the patio were perfect for her arts and crafts, and the fresh peach color of the two-story house made everything look cheerful and welcoming. This morning, Tricia's father had set up their old camping tent for their "magic carpet ride."

"I want a drink of water, water . . . water," Amanda clammered. She stopped at the tile water faucet at the end of the breezeway, and Butterscotch, the Bennetts' cat, rubbed against her legs as she took a long, long drink.

"Come on," Becky told her sister. As president of the club, she should be early to be sure everything was on target.

"Morning!" she called out to her friends, who had just stepped out of the back door.

"Good morning, Becky and Amanda," Tricia, Cara, and Melanie chorused loudly. "Welcome to Morning Fun for Kids!"

"Come on! Who are you trying to impress?" Becky asked.

Laughing, they headed for the picnic table to work out the day's schedule, as usual.

"Ready to go camping again?" Tricia asked.

"No way!" Becky answered. "I suppose you're going to pull El Froggo on the Funners."

"I am," Tricia said, grinning. She already knew of El Froggo's "success" on the camping trip. "You might say that old El Froggo is a talented tent collapser."

Becky remembered to lighten up. "That you could."

Just then, Jess arrived in the backyard. Last night, she'd returned from Catalina Island, where she'd been with her family since Monday. "How'd the camping trip go, Becky?"

"Don't ask," Becky replied. "Mom is now wearing an engagement ring—"

"Whoa!" Jess exclaimed.

Before Jess could say more, Becky said, "I need help . . .

besides, Mom wants you all to work at the wedding reception—"

"Sounds serious, all right," Jess said.

"Afraid it is. Let's talk this afternoon at the meeting." She recalled not too long ago when she hadn't wanted to talk about Mom and Mr. Bradshaw to anyone.

Amanda glanced at her suspiciously, then went inside to play with Bryan. At the picnic table, Becky picked up the day's schedule, which read,

AFTER PARENTS SIGN THE KIDS IN:

1. Magic carpet (Tricia. Others to guide Funners into tent and help with red bandanas.)
2. Camping pictures (Becky)
3. Camping crafts (Melanie and Jess)
4. Midmorning snacks (Cara)
5. Gymnastics (Jess)
6. Free time for swings (all in charge)

It sounded like plenty to keep the Funners busy for three hours, Becky thought. She just wished she didn't have to be reminded of the camping trip.

Minutes before nine o'clock, they heard a car pulling up in front of the house, then car doors slamming. Funners arriving. That was almost sure.

"Where's the sign-in clipboard?" Becky asked as a knock sounded on the gate. "I see it!" She grabbed the clipboard from the redwood table and dashed to the breezeway gate.

When she opened it, Mrs. Davis stood smiling with Jimjim and Jojo, whose eyes were even greener than Amanda's, and far more mischievous.

"Well, look who's here!" Becky said as if they'd never attended Morning Fun for Kids.

Mrs. Davis laughed and began to fill out the clipboard form that said: FUNNER'S NAME, AGE, TIME IN, TIME OUT, PARENTS' PHONE, DOCTOR'S NAME/PHONE NUMBER. Next, Becky handed Mrs. Davis two name tags for each of the boys, to be worn on the fronts and backs of their shirts.

"I hear your mother's getting married again," Mrs. Davis remarked. She looked pleased, as if it were happy news.

Not if I have anything to do with it! Becky thought grimly.

"Well . . ." Mrs. Davis went on with a little frown, "have a great morning."

"We will," Becky assured her. "Jimjim and Jojo always seem to have fun."

"That they do," Mrs. Davis agreed.

Out front, more cars were pulling up, and a lot of car doors were slamming. As usual, Friday would probably be a big day for them since moms liked to leave their kids here while they did their weekend shopping.

Jojo and Jimjim saw the tent and raced toward it.

"Not yet!" Cara warned them, intercepting them just in time. "The tent's going to be a surprise. Let me give you a ride on the swings instead."

Moments later, they were riding high in the swings, with Cara pushing. "Go! Go!" the boys yelled, then added in their secret twin language, "Umpty-dumpty-dum-dum! Umpty-dumpel-um-lum-a-dum-dum!"

Tricia, Jess, and Melanie were greeting kids and parents at the gate, and Becky hurried back herself. It looked as if, this morning, everyone was arriving at once.

By nine-fifteen, thirteen little kids—including Amanda,

and Bryan and Suzanne Bennett—filled the yard. Becky whispered to Tricia, "Let's hope no more come!"

"You know it," Tricia answered. As they rolled out the big, raggedy brown rug, she announced, "All right, all of you Funners, we're going to go up to the mountains this morning . . . up to the mountains so we can go camping."

The Funners came running, then plopped down on the familiar rug, excited.

Tricia stood at the end of the rug and raised her hands dramatically. "We are going to z-o-o-m a-w-a-y on our m-a-g-i-c c-a-r-p-e-t," she announced as the Funners settled on it. She told the other TCC members, "Let's hand out the cowboy bandanas and help the Funners with them so we're ready to f-l-y! We need the bandanas over their eyes."

Becky helped the others tie the red bandanas over the Funners' eyes, remembering her family's camping disaster in the windstorm. She'd told Tricia all about it, and no doubt Tricia would use it in today's magic carpet story.

It'd be a wonder if Tricia could outdo some of their other exciting magic carpet adventures, like the day of the Chinese dragon, but knowing her, anything was possible. She wore her green shorts and green Tee, which looked great with her reddish blond hair, and she called out a super dramatic, "Now everyone ready so we can f-l-y . . . f-l-y . . . f-l-y!

"Let's tell our names now!" she added. "I'm Tricia!"

"Sam Miller!" yelled one boy.

"Craig Leonard!" shouted another.

In moments, all the Funners had called out their names, which they knew was important for magic carpet flying.

"Don't take those bandanas away from your eyes," Tricia warned them. "We're t-a-k-i-n-g o-f-f over Santa Rosita. Can't you just imagine our houses as we zoom past over their roofs! And now we're flying over our airport . . . yiiiiii! . . . watch out for those airplanes! Let's go higher! Yiiiii!"

"Harrrroooom, harrrroooom!" Sam Miller yelled.

"And there in the distance, you can see the d-e-s-e-r-t with lots and lots of s-a-n-d and c-a-c-t-u-s . . . and farther away and higher, you can see the m-o-u-n-t-a-i-n-s and then the f-o-r-e-s-t. Look! It's a red-tailed hawk gliding by us . . . and there's an e-a-g-l-e!"

Becky waited with the other girls as Tricia continued the imaginary ride. The plan was, when Tricia told them, to guide the Funners to the tent with the bandanas over their eyes.

"W-a-t-c-h o-u-t for those c-l-o-u-d-s!"

"Zoom!" someone yelled. "Harroooommmmmm!"

"Now we're going to do something v-e-r-y s-p-e-c-i-a-l," Tricia told them. She signaled the TCC girls to slowly guide the Funners to the tent. "All right, Funners, s-t-a-n-d u-p c-a-r-e-f-u-l-l-y o-n t-h-e m-a-g-i-c c-a-r-p-e-t. You're going to be guided down into our campground as we land. Keep your bandanas over your eyes till we get there. We'll help you. Put your hands on each others' shoulders and f-o-l-l-o-w the Funner in front of you."

Becky and the others guided the Funners' hands to each others' shoulders until they stood in a line.

"Now, let's hear some z-o-o-m-i-n-g," Tricia told them. "We'll fly a little way, and then we'll sit down."

Becky wondered if the Funners really thought they'd be flying as they trooped forward, hands on each others' shoulders. Tricia led them around until they were all in the tent.

"Now," Tricia said, "F-u-n-n-e-r-s and g-u-i-d-e-s, you may s-i-t d-o-w-n."

Becky closed the tent flap, making it darker.

"Now," Tricia said, "F-u-n-n-e-r-s, t-a-k-e d-o-w-n y-o-u-r b-a-n-d-a-n-a-s."

"Whoa!" Sam Miller said. "It looks like we're camping!"

"We are," Tricia told them, turning on a battery-powered lantern. "We are camping up in the mountains. Let's sing some good camping songs."

Becky felt like shaking her head. God had surely given Tricia a talent for acting and storytelling. It really seemed that they were out camping somewhere.

It didn't take long for Tricia to teach them the chorus, "Oh, we're camping, we're camping, on the old campgrounds. . . ." After that, she sang the verses, and everyone joined in the "Oh, we're camping, we're camping, on the old campgrounds."

Next, they sang "The Camptown Races," which didn't have anything to do with camping, but sounded like it did in the lantern-lit tent. Then, "Row, Row, Row Your Boat."

They'd been singing for some time when Tricia picked up a sleeping bag. She said, puzzled, "Well, look at the big lump in this sleeping bag! I wouldn't want to sleep on that, would you? I wonder what it is. . . ?"

Becky knew exactly what it was, and what would happen when Tricia opened the bag. How could she ever forget?

Suddenly El Froggo sprang out of the sleeping bag, almost hitting the tent roof.

The Funners screamed, and Tricia called out, "Whoa! It's a good camping trick, isn't it?" She hurried over to pick him up. Holding him for all to see, she said, "May I introduce my friend, E-l F-r-o-g-g-o. Can't he jump?"

"Yeah!" the Funners yelled. "Make him jump again!"

El Froggo jumped again and again in the tent, making the

Funners squeal with excitement.

It was more fun going camping with the Funners than it had been on the real camping trip, Becky decided. At least here, El Froggo hadn't made such a fool of her. Besides, a magic carpet ride to go camping was a lot less trouble than riding along forever on the real trip to the mountains with the Bradshaws. And, here, in her imagination, there were no engagement rings or wedding plans.

That afternoon, when Becky called the TCC meeting to order, she had something more important in mind than just hearing the minutes of the meeting and the treasurer's report. Sitting in Jess's desk chair, she pounded the desk with her hand for order. What she had to do was try to enlist them to help her to stop the big event, which was getting closer.

When the old and new business had been discussed, Becky said, "I have some business to talk about now. You . . . ah . . . all know about Mom's engagement and upcoming wedding. And you're all booked to serve at her wedding reception at church for two hours—"

"It's going to be fun," Tricia began.

Becky drew a deep breath and said, "Not for me." She didn't know how to bring up her problem, so she just said, "At the engagement party tomorrow night, at Mrs. Llewellyn's . . . I . . . well, I need your help. You've been talking about us helping each other, and now I really need it. Maybe you don't know it yet, but I don't want Mom to marry Mr. Bradshaw or anyone else, for that matter."

Their eyes widened, and she hurried on. "I've got to do

something at the party to make them mad at each other, and you've got to help me."

Jess had been doing side stretches on the closest blue floor mat, but now she stopped. "What do you plan to do?"

"I don't know yet," Becky admitted. "I was hoping some of you might have ideas."

They all stared at each other. Silence.

"Maybe you could just tell them that you don't want them to get married," Jess suggested.

"I think they already know that."

Tricia shook her head, her reddish blond hair swinging over her shoulders. "I don't know, Becky. As much as I'd miss you not living next door, I think it might be all right for your mom to marry Mr. Bradshaw."

"All right?!" Becky gasped. "Tricia Bennett, I thought you were my friend!"

"Sorry," Tricia replied, truly looking like she was. "But I'm not the only one who thinks it's a good idea."

"Probably your mom does!" Becky said. "Besides, she's on Mom's side because she's her best friend!"

Tricia shrugged.

"What about Quinn Bradshaw?" Cara suggested. "You thought he didn't want them to get married, either. Maybe you could talk to him about it."

"I don't know. . . . I don't think he likes me much. When we went camping, he flapped a fish out of the water right at me. On purpose. Then he hooked my new jeweled visor with his fishing rod and flung it into the stream. It's ruined, absolutely ruined. And he thought it was funny."

"I tried to get something on him from my brothers," Jess said. "All they could think of was that Quinn's president of the chess and the science club . . . and, well, they say that he's a brain and a loner. The only interesting thing is he's sort of morbid. You know, he likes dissecting frogs and all of that disgusting stuff."

"Maybe he'll be a hospital pathologist," Melanie said, "you know, the ones who study dead bodies."

"Yurks!" Becky said.

"Or maybe a mortician!" Jess added. "You know, the ones at funeral homes."

Becky swallowed hard. "Well, I don't care what he'll be! Right now, I just need someone to do something at the engagement party. Preferably something terrible. And my only hope is with you guys."

"But what if it ruins our club's reputation?" Cara asked.

Becky almost didn't care. Almost.

They sat on Jess's beds thinking and thinking, but no one could come up with anything reasonable.

The phone rang.

As Tricia picked it up, Jess was saying, "Well, we'll be at Mrs. Llewellyn's tonight. And with Mrs. Llewellyn, a-n-y-t-h-i-n-g is possible."

I hope so! Becky thought. But hoping hadn't been helpful so far. She sure didn't want to, but since her friends were no help, maybe she'd phone Quinn Bradshaw.

CHAPTER

8

When Becky arrived home from the meeting, Amanda was in the bathtub, and Mom was dressing for the engagement party. The only good news was that the red roses Mr. Bradshaw had given Mom last week had dropped shriveled petals on the dining area table. Maybe the big romance could still die like the rose petals, Becky hoped.

"Your clothes are out on your bed, Beck," Mom called out from her room.

"You put my clothes out?!" Becky echoed.

"I thought it was the wisest thing to do for tonight. I thought you might forget to wear your new white dress."

Hmmmpphhh! Becky thought, furious. *Mom getting my clothes out is really too much!*

Instead of going to her room, she turned back to the living room. Something had to be done.

Quite suddenly she remembered what Willie Lin had done

for Melanie's birthday party and a great idea hit.

She hurried to the kitchen and checked out the Bradshaw phone number. Not surprisingly, Mom had written it in red and underlined it. Becky grabbed the phone and punched in the number. If Mr. Bradshaw answered, she'd just hang up.

The phone began to ring at their house and, on the third ring, a male voice said, "Hello."

Not Mr. Bradshaw, she guessed. "Quinn?"

"Just a minute," whoever it was replied. Then he yelled, "Quinn, it's for you! It's a girl! A girl actually calling *you*, Quinn!"

Next came a curious, "Hello? This is Quintin Bradshaw."

Quintin?! Becky thought. *Quintin!* But she cupped her hand around the phone. "Hi, Quinn. It's me, Becky Hamilton."

He sounded disappointed. "Oh."

"I—I'm calling because . . . I thought maybe you feel the same as I do. . . ."

"To what are you referring?" he asked, suspicious.

"I'm calling about the wedding. I thought maybe you'd like to . . . stop it, too."

"A correct assumption," he replied. He paused. "What kind of a scheme have you concocted?"

She hesitated. "Promise not to tell?"

He drew a resigned breath. "If necessary."

As long as she'd gone this far, Becky decided to go on. "First of all, Mom hates bugs and snakes—"

"So?" he asked.

"Well, yesterday when I was cleaning house with the Twelve Candles girls at Mrs. Llewellyn's, she told us she's giving our parents an engagement present. I guess other people might bring presents, too. I thought . . . maybe you could—" She swallowed hard. ". . . maybe you could put Julius Squeezer in a box and wrap it up like an engagement present. Mom would open it and be so upset that she'd get mad at your father. It's not a perfect idea, but I can't think of anything else. Maybe you can think of something better. . . ?"

Quinn's brain must have been whirring because he didn't answer immediately. "I'll consider it," he finally said. Then, without as much as a goodbye, he hung up the phone.

So much for Quinn Bradshaw's manners! Becky thought as she put down the phone herself. Still, he was considering her idea, and he was supposed to be a brain. As she made her way to her room to get dressed, she wondered what he might do.

At six thirty, the doorbell rang.

"Becky, will you get it?" Mom called from her room. "It's probably Paul."

"I'll go, too," Amanda offered. She looked cute in her new pale green summer dress, white tights, and sandals. "Come on," she told Becky. "I bet it's Mr. Bradshaw."

But when they opened the door, no one was there.

Instead, a small box from Santa Rosita Flowers lay on the doormat. "To Libby Bennett," it said.

Becky brought it in. "A box from Santa Rosita Flowers!" she yelled down the hallway to her mother. "Looks like it must be a corsage for you."

"Let me see!" Mom said, hurrying into the living room. She wore her silky blue-green dress that matched her eyes, and her dark hair was up in a French twist. Taking the box, she beamed. "It must be a corsage from Paul . . . or maybe from the Llewellyns. It's the sort of thing they would do."

Mom took off the white bow, them removed the box's lid. Looking inside, she let out a piercing shriek.

She dropped the box, and when it hit, a huge hairy spider fell onto the living room carpet.

"A tarantula!" she yelled.

Landing upside down, the hairy tarantula slowly turned itself over, and began to crawl toward the door.

"Ohhhhhh! Who'd do that?" Mom asked, backing away.

Quinn, Becky thought, shuddering. *Quinn would do it.*

Suddenly a knowing light came into Mom's eyes. She pressed her lips together, then said, "It's probably supposed to be funny, but I certainly don't see much humor in scaring someone with a tarantula. Amanda, please get the broom."

Before long, the tarantula had been swept out the door and into the front yard, where it crept away under the bushes.

Minutes later, when they saw Mr. Bradshaw drive up, Mom warned, "Don't say a word about the tarantula to him."

"Why not?" Amanda asked.

"Because I asked you not to," Mom answered firmly. She hurried to open the door for Mr. Bradshaw.

He stood in the doorway, holding another bouquet of red roses and beaming at her. "Don't you look beautiful!" he remarked, as usual. Then squeezing her hand, he presented the roses.

"Thank you, Paul. And thank you for the roses. You shouldn't—"

"But I want to," he objected, still beaming at her.

"You look very nice yourself," Mom told him.

It was true; he did look nice in his navy blue suit.

"That blue-gray necktie matches your eyes," Mom told

him, "and your suit matches your car."

"So it does," he said with a chuckle. He stepped from the small entry into the living room.

"I'll put the roses into a vase," Mom told him. She hurried off toward the kitchen, picking up the vase of dying roses on her way through the dining area.

"Well, well, don't you two look beautiful, too," he said to Becky and Amanda.

Amanda twirled around to show off her dress, but Becky didn't even look down at her white dress. She just answered with a plain, "Thank you, Mr. Bradshaw."

He hesitated, then said, "You know, girls, I'd really like it if you could call me something else besides 'Mister Bradshaw.' I sense you don't want to call me Dad, because I'm not your real father and you still love him." He looked hopeful. "Do you think you could call me Paul?"

Becky considered it, then shook her head. "I don't think so, Mr. Bradshaw."

Amanda blinked, taking it all in. Then she grinned at him. "You know what I want to call you? I want to call you Paw-paw . . . you know, like Paul-Paul . . . Paw-paw."

He gave a delighted laugh, and just then, Mom came into the dining area with the fresh red roses in a vase. "Did you hear that?" he asked. "Amanda wants to call me Paw-paw!"

Mom gave a laugh. "It's fine with me if you like it."

"I never expected to be called by that particular name, but I think I'm going to like it very much," he said.

"Paw-paw . . . Paw-paw . . . Paw-paw!" Amanda sang out, dancing all around them.

How could she forget our real father so quickly? Becky thought, her heart hurting. Of course, Amanda remembered him mostly from pictures, since she had only been three when he died.

Mom snatched up her white evening purse. "We're ready, I think," she said, and Mr. Bradshaw opened the door for them.

Outside, Becky noticed that the tarantula was gone. If Quinn thought a tarantula was enough to discourage Mom, he'd sure thought wrong.

At exactly seven o'clock, they drove into the Llewellyns' circular drive in Mr. Bradshaw's dark blue Cadillac.

"Good," Mom said, "we're the first ones here." She gave a light laugh and turned a fond glance at Mr. Bradshaw. "I can't quite believe that there's an engagement party tonight for us. Everything is rushing along so quickly."

You know it! Becky thought. Far too quickly to suit her. Nervous, she eyed the impressive, ultra-modern white stucco house that rose two stories high in front and three stories in the backyard; by the wide double-door entry, huge pots held trailing red geraniums. Suddenly Becky had a thought. Maybe Mrs. Llewellyn could still be enlisted to stop the wedding.

As Becky made her way to the front steps, she cast a glance through the pine trees toward the Bradshaw house next door. No sign of Quinn.

Mrs. Llewellyn opened the double doors dramatically and, beaming, scrutinized everyone through her thick glasses. "Oh, don't you all look wonderful, just wonderful?!" she exclaimed in her excited, squawky voice. She flapped her hands as she spoke. "Come in! Do come in!"

Her frazzled hair was redder than ever, and she wore an expensive-looking sequined white dress. Lulu, the cocker spaniel bustling around her feet, matched her hair, since she was a reddish color, too. She was such a spoiled dog that she didn't even bother to bark anymore.

"What an honor it is for us to host your engagement party!" Mrs. L. was saying. "Why, Mr. Llewellyn and I have just been discussing how honored we are. . . . Now, where's that wonderful husband of mine? Ah, here he comes now."

Mr. Llewellyn, a short, gray-haired man, strolled into the grand entryway and smiled at them. "Welcome!" he said, excited. "Welcome!" He sounded a little like his wife, except his voice was deeper. "It is indeed an honor to host your engagement party," he told Mom and Mr. Bradshaw. "I hope you'll be as happy as my dear wife and I have been these many years."

Becky felt like crossing her eyes. A big help they were—encouraging Mom and Mr. Bradshaw, when what she needed was exactly the opposite.

Inside, the Llewellyns escorted them past the huge plants and modern sculptures to the living room. "Mrs. Wurtzel is catering our dinner, as usual," Mrs. L. explained, then rushed on. "The other Twelve Candles girls are in the kitchen, getting ready to help serve. We'll dine on Mrs. Wurtzel's fine beef *Provencal* out on the patio. And I've planned to have you lovebirds open the gifts out there, too. Now, I know you've requested no wedding gifts, so I've told everyone that engagement presents are in order."

"You didn't—" Mom began.

Mrs. L. gave a laugh. "Of course, I did. Oh, I do love seeing gifts opened at a party!"

Becky thought she must have looked peculiar because Mrs. L. spoke directly to her. "Well, my dear, for once you'll be among those of us who are served instead of doing the serving."

Becky nodded.

Lulu Llewellyn was wagging her tail and now she came to rub against Becky's legs.

"Look," Mrs. L. said, "Lulu remembers you so fondly."

Probably from the infamous pizza invitation chase, Becky thought, giving Lulu a nervous glance.

"Oh, I do believe I'm jealous," Mrs. L. gushed. "Just look at how my Lulu loves you!"

As they all settled on the luxurious white couches, Mrs. L. confided, "We're having nothing but romantic music tonight on our new CD player . . . nothing but romance. Oh, I do love romantic parties and weddings!"

Ugh, Becky thought. Mrs. L. would be no help at all.

Becky spotted Jess and Tricia bringing silver trays of hors d'oeuvres into the living room. And here came Cara and Melanie with trays holding cups of pink punch. They looked perfect in their white skirts and blouses, and the gold TCC candle medallions around their necks. When they grinned at her, Becky gave in and crossed her eyes, making them almost break down with laughter.

Before long, neighbors and friends arrived, including Gram and Reverend and Mrs. Meyer from their church. The Twelve Candles girls took the guests' gifts out to a table on the patio. Like the romantic music, grown-ups soon filled the living room. Some wandered out to the midlevel patio, standing by the wrought-iron railing and looking down at the trees below.

Finally, the Bradshaw boys arrived.

Becky was glad to see Quinn hand a box to Cara. A long, narrow white box with a white bow. He glanced into the living room, saw Becky, and gave a nod. Was there hope after all?

"And here come those fine Bradshaw boys!" Mrs. L. announced. "What a pleasure it is to have had them as neighbors these many years. They have grown into fine young men before our very eyes."

The boys wore suits, and smiled uncomfortably.

Becky noticed Mrs. L. give Quinn a suspicious look before she added, "What fine, fine boys."

At last, most of the guests had arrived, and Becky watched her friends rush dishes of food out to the patio. She decided it'd be more fun to be helping them than it was to make small talk with adults.

After a while, Mrs. L. clapped her hands, then said, "I do believe that everyone's here. If you'll all stand, I'd like to propose a toast to our lovebirds, Libby and Paul! May you always be as happy as you are now!"

Lovebirds, uffff! Becky thought as the other guests raised their punch cups and called out, "Hear, hear!" "Best wishes!" and "To Libby and Paul!"

Moments later, Mrs. L. announced, "We're ready for dinner. If you'll all go to the patio, I have name cards out at the tables for seating."

Next, Reverend Meyer offered a prayer. "Father God, we ask you to bless this couple who dream tonight of a bright future together. And we thank you for this nourishment. . . ."

Outside on the huge patio, five round tables covered with white tablecloths were set with gleaming goblets and silverware. On the way to the buffet, Becky glanced at the name cards. Mom and Mr. Bradshaw would sit with Gram, the Llewellyns, and the Meyers; she and Amanda had to sit with the Bradshaw boys and three other Bradshaws. Near their table was the lace-covered gift table. Thinking of Quinn's box, at least, made her hopeful.

At dinner, the other Bradshaws at the table turned out to

be two of Mr. Bradshaw's grown-up nephews—Jeffrey and Craig—and the red-haired lady was Jeffrey's wife. Mrs. Bradshaw questioned Becky about the Twelve Candles Club, then asked her to baby-sit on Sunday night. With Mom and Mr. Bradshaw at the next table, Becky felt as if she had to be polite and give in.

Jonathan and Charlie Bradshaw made polite conversation with her, too, and Gram visited a little from the next table. But Quinn didn't say a word to her. Only once, when everyone else was talking, he muttered, "How'd the florist box go?"

"Didn't work," she muttered back.

"Just wait," he whispered with a glance toward the gift table. "Just wait."

She was waiting, all right, and now Lulu had planted herself on Becky's feet. No matter how she moved her feet, Lulu wanted to rest on them for a pillow. Lulu was heavy and hot. It seemed forever before the TCC girls had cleared the table and served the coffee and chocolate cheesecake.

Finally, Mrs. Llewellyn stood and clapped her hands again for attention. "And now I'll ask our lovebirds to open their gifts. Oh, I do so love gift openings."

Quinn shot Becky a pleased look.

Mrs. L. handed the gifts to Mom and Mr. Bradshaw, who opened them together. Everyone exclaimed over the vases, candlesticks, and silver trays.

Mrs. L. handed Quinn's long, narrow white box to Mom, and Becky tensed. Suddenly she remembered how El Froggo had scared her, jumping out, and she realized what a serious thing it could be to find a real snake in a gift box. She couldn't help rising to her feet to warn Mom.

Just then Mr. Bradshaw removed the lid, and Julius

Squeezer raised up. As he slithered from the box, Mom screamed and flung herself into Mr. Bradshaw's arms—right into his arms in front of everyone!

Mrs. L. gave a fierce shriek, gripping Mr. L.'s arm as if she might faint. Lulu jumped up and, barking her way through people's legs, chased Julius, who quickly slithered off the patio onto a nearby tree, then down to the ground.

"Ohhhh . . . ohhhh . . . ohhhhh!!!" Mrs. Llewellyn called out. "Lulu, come back! Ohhhh. . . . Who could possibly do such a dastardly deed?"

Having asked the question, she slowly turned to face Quinn, who was at that very moment swinging down over the wrought-iron patio railing into the tree, chasing Julius.

"Quinn!" Mr. Bradshaw shouted. "Just wait until I get ahold of you!"

Becky turned away, a terrible tightness in her chest.

Probably Quinn would tell on her, and her great idea had slithered away. Worse, Mom was in Mr. Bradshaw's arms as if he were a hero. Becky knew she'd have to come up with something else—and soon.

CHAPTER 9

The next morning, Becky was the first one out of bed. Saturday, she reminded herself. Car washing morning. She dressed in her old blue Tee and cut-offs, grabbed a granola bar in the kitchen, and hurried out into the garage before Mom could nail her about the snake.

She'd just pressed the garage door opener and was climbing onto her bike when Mom opened the kitchen door. Her hair was a little wild and she wore her robe, so she'd just gotten up. "Have fun!" she called out.

"Thanks," Becky answered glumly.

She darted another glance at her mother. Why wasn't she mad about last night? Didn't she guess Becky was part of Quinn's plan to put Julius in the gift box? Mom hadn't even mentioned it. Instead, she'd talked about how nice the Llewellyns' party had been. She was perfectly pleasant.

"If I'm not home at noon," Mom said, "I'll be out picking

up my wedding dress and checking on the wedding flowers."

Becky mumbled an "okay" as she rode out of the garage.

"I'll close the garage door," Mom told her, then pressed the garage door button.

As the garage door ground down, Becky rode next door to Tricia's house. She stopped in front of the Bennetts' garage and tore open her granola bar.

"Tricia?" she called up.

Tricia opened her upstairs window and stuck her head out. "Whoa, you're early! Wait just a minute. I'll be right down."

Becky stood straddling her bike in the morning sunshine, chewing the granola bar. It occurred to her again that Mom didn't tell her anything anymore, not like she'd done before she and Mr. Bradshaw had become serious. Now the two of them seemed "thick as thieves," as Gram called it. Full of secrets.

The thought prompted a brainstorm.

Tomorrow when she baby-sat the Jeffrey Bradshaws' kids, maybe she could find out something secret about Mr. Bradshaw. Get something on him, like Jess had tried to get on Quinn.

Just then Tricia's garage door ground upward, and Tricia rode out on her bike. "What a good party at the Llewellyns' last night!" she said. "Especially when they opened the presents! What did your mom say about the snake?"

"Nothing," Becky answered.

"Nothing?!"

"Absolutely nothing. I think maybe she's too busy thinking about wedding plans," Becky decided.

"Hmmmm, that must be it," Tricia answered as they rode off toward the Hutchinsons' house. She shook her head. "But it strikes me as very p-e-c-u-l-i-a-r."

They didn't wait for Melanie because she had a tryout for a modeling job this morning. As they rode along the street, Tricia cast a glance at her. "You feeling any better about the wedding?"

"No way!" Becky answered. "And I don't want to talk about it, either! I'm not even going to think about it!"

Nothing exciting—or even interesting—happened all morning, but after lunch, a letter arrived from her grandparents, Nana and Gramp Hamilton in Indiana. Amazingly, it was addressed to her. She ripped open the envelope and read,

> Dear Becky,
>
> We wanted to write to you especially because we suspect your mother's wedding might be difficult for you. We want you to know that we're supportive of your mother's plan. She loved our son very much and deserves to find such happiness again. We encourage you to accept Paul Bradshaw—not as a replacement for your father—but as someone who could be a very special friend. . . .

Becky couldn't bear to read on and stuffed the letter into a desk drawer, tears streaming down her face. Was it true? Did her mom deserve happiness again? Could Mr. Bradshaw be a friend? . . . Oh, she didn't even want to think about it.

That night, when Mom was out with Mr. Bradshaw, Becky opened her closet to choose an outfit for Sunday school. A pale blue silk dress hung in her closet, with a plastic clothing bag over it. Her maid of honor dress for the wedding!

Amanda had been hanging around her all evening. "Isn't it beautiful?" she remarked, her head in the doorway. "Mine is yellow and it's beautiful, too."

Becky glanced at the dress again, and had to admit it was the prettiest dress she'd ever seen. Feeling like a traitor, she slammed her closet door shut. "Shut up!" she snapped at her sister, and immediately felt guilty.

Oh, God, she prayed, *I hate myself like this. Help me!*

The next morning, when Mom drove Becky and Amanda to church, she still hadn't mentioned the Julius Squeezer episode. Instead, she was full of plans for having lunch at the Bradshaws', where they'd discuss the final redecorating plans with Gram.

"Are you sure you don't want to discuss your bedroom?" Mom asked Becky.

Becky sat in the backseat of the car again, and she just shook her head, since Mom was looking at her in the car's rearview mirror. At least she wouldn't have to go to the Bradshaws' for lunch. The plan was for her to ride home from church with the Bennetts.

"Then your room there will be decorated as close as Gram can make it to your present room," Mom said.

"Fine," Becky answered, shrugging.

Amanda turned from the front seat to look at her, and Mom darted another glance at her in the rearview mirror. "Oh, Becky," she said, "I wish you'd turn back into my sweet daughter again."

Becky clamped her mouth shut.

Mom turned her attention back to driving. After a while she asked, "What will you do at home alone this afternoon?"

"I don't know. Don't forget, I'm baby-sitting tonight for the Jeffrey Bradshaws. They're picking me up at five o'clock."

"I assume we'll be home by then," Mom said. "We have a lot of final plans to make."

"I'll be all right," Becky told her. "And I'll be sure to lock up the house behind me," she added as a reminder that she was almost always responsible.

At church, she trudged to the youth room alone. Even the red geraniums blooming around the bright green lawn didn't seem cheerful this morning.

"Hey-hey, Becky!" Bear called out as she came into the youth room. As usual, he wore a wildly flowered shirt and baggy cotton pants, and he was adjusting the strings on his guitar. He said to her, "You're looking good."

She gave him a little smile. Only a few kids sat in the tan folding chairs, and they were talking to each other, so Becky sat down alone.

Bear ambled over to her, carrying his guitar. His blue eyes filled with concern. "You want to be alone?"

She shrugged.

"You want to talk?" he asked.

She shrugged again.

"Maybe you want to talk to God," Bear suggested. "That's what I do when I'm feeling down."

She must have looked surprised, because he added, "Yep, your old friend Bear is human, too. I can let problems get me down, just like anyone else, but God doesn't want me down there. He wants me full of love and joy and praising Him."

"I've prayed about it," Becky said. She stared at a big yellow flower on his shirt. Actually, she hadn't prayed much at all.

Bear raised his bushy brows. "Since your mom is getting

married here next Saturday, it's my guess you're concerned about changes ahead."

She nodded, sudden tears pressing against her eyes.

"You want me to pray with you now?" Bear asked.

She nodded again.

"Let's bow our heads," he said, guitar still in hand.

He hesitated, then quietly prayed, "Dear Heavenly Father, we come before you feeling a little unsure today. It's not easy to have our lives changing all around us, to think about having a whole new family. We do know, though, that you want the very best for us. In the Bible it says that your eye is on the sparrow, caring about him, and we know you care at least that much about every single one of us. We pray that you'd give Becky the peace that being in your will brings. We pray in the blessed name of Jesus. Amen."

Becky opened her eyes. "Thanks."

"I'll keep praying for you," he said.

She couldn't say she felt any better, but she did feel good about Bear's prayer. She needed to feel peaceful. As it was, the room was filling up, and here came her friends. With Bear praying for her, probably everyone would know she was in some kind of trouble.

When all of the kids were seated, Bear strummed his guitar for attention, then said his usual, "Good morning, gang!"

"Good morning, Bear!" the group echoed.

They looked around the room for new kids, but there were none to introduce, and no birthdays this week, either.

Bear strummed his guitar for quiet again, then gave the announcements. That over, he said, "Last Sunday we talked about Jesus being the light of this world and that we're supposed to walk in that light so we can shed it around the world for Him. Remember we said, 'Lighten up'? How many of you really did lighten up the lives of people around you last week? Let's see a show of hands."

Not a single hand went up.

"How many of you tried just a little to lighten lives up?" he asked.

A few hands went up, but Becky couldn't raise hers. She'd done just the opposite. She'd cast gloom and darkness wherever she'd been.

"It sounds as if we've been crowding Jesus out of our lives," Bear said. "You know it's really dumb, a no-brainer, to backslide . . . to get away from the Lord. It takes away our joy and, in the end, it usually makes us miserable."

Tricia and Melanie darted glances at her, and Becky closed her eyes. Did they think she was a backslider? Well, whether they did or not, it was becoming clearer and clearer that all four of the TCC girls were for Mom and Mr. Bradshaw's wedding. They cared more about it than they cared about her!

Bear went on. "Since so few of you raised your hands, let's start with the perfect song, 'Come into My Heart.' "

Becky remembered singing it. She'd meant the words then, but now her voice trembled and the words seemed all jumbled as she joined in with the others. "Come into my heart, Lord Jesus . . . come into my heart. . . ."

Had she been crowding Him out of her heart? she wondered. No, others—like Mom and Mr. Bradshaw—had been crowding Him out for her! That was their fault, not hers.

Next, Bear led them as they sang, "Give Me Peace, Peace, Wonderful Peace," and slowly, very slowly, Becky began to feel more peaceful.

Becky was just driving away from her house with Mr. Jeffrey Bradshaw when she saw Mom's green Oldsmobile coming down La Crescenta. Probably they'd had a wonderful time with their stupid redecorating plans, she thought, and they'd come back late so they didn't have to face her!

Mom honked the car horn, but Becky ignored it.

Mr. Jeffrey Bradshaw gave her a peculiar look, as if he'd recognized Mom, and Becky made herself smile innocently at him. Best to be bright and cheerful. He'd already asked her to call him Jeffrey.

"Well," he said now, "I hope you'll like my three boys. I . . . er . . . I'm afraid they can be a bit wild at times."

"Wild?" Becky repeated.

He had a bushy dark mustache, which lifted as he smiled at her. "Just a little." Steering with one hand, he ran the other through his equally bushy dark hair. "You've got to be sure to let them know you're in charge right from the beginning. I guess I shouldn't admit it, but some of our baby-sitters have had trouble."

Wonderful, Becky thought. *Just wonderful.*

Now that she considered it, she wasn't surprised. That's why she'd been asked to baby-sit with almost no notice: These parents were desperate for a sitter. Wild kids were just what she needed when everything else in her life was going wrong.

They rode along in silence again.

Finally, as they turned down Ocean Avenue, Jeffrey said, "Philip is nine. He's the oldest, and he likes to be in charge. Oliver is eight and a little rebellious. What I mean is he generally tries to do the opposite of what you tell him. And Jackmon, the baby, is a two-and-a-half-year-old. Mostly he says no."

"Philip, Oliver, and Jackmon," Becky said. Best to start learning their names right away. And if she was going to pry information out of the older two about Mr. Paul Bradshaw, she'd better learn everything else she could about the boys. She asked, "Do Philip and Oliver look alike?"

"Not at all," Jeffrey answered. "Philip is taller and dark-haired like me. Oliver is redheaded and curly haired like his mother."

When they pulled up in front of their yellow stucco house, the three boys were already peering out a downstairs window.

"There they are watching for us now," Jeffrey said, parking the car. He cast an uneasy glance at her. "Hope I haven't made you nervous about them. Emily, my wife, says I talk too much."

Becky just smiled a little.

Philip, Oliver, and Jackmon.

Inside, Emily wore a pretty pink dress for their evening out, and she definitely looked ready to escape the house. "We're so glad you could sit, and we can have a night out," she told Becky.

Becky nodded. "Here's the Twelve Candles Club Baby-Sitting Safety Checklist. We ask that our clients fill it out, then show us how all of the doors and windows lock. Also, the children's rooms, and where the fire extinguishers are."

"Good idea," Emily said. "This way."

She headed into the kitchen for a pencil, then began to write down answers to the safety checklist questions. "While I'm finishing this, my husband can show you about the doors, windows, and fire extinguishers."

Becky saw the boys watching her closely.

They followed along with her and their father. "You must

be Philip," Becky said to the taller, dark-haired boy.

"How'd you know?" he demanded.

"You're Oliver," she told the curly haired redhead.

"How'd you know that?" Oliver asked.

"You're Jackmon," she told the two-and-a-half-year-old.

"No!" Jackmon objected. "No!"

"Jackmon!" their father warned. "You know very well that's your name. Now this is Becky Hamilton, and she's not only going to be your baby-sitter tonight, but sort of a distant cousin. I expect you all to be very good to her so she'll want to come baby-sit here again."

The older boys were frowning at her, and Jackmon shouted another, "No!"

Becky couldn't help thinking that with the grouchy look on Jackmon's face, he looked like a pint-sized Brutus from the Popeye cartoon. Only this Brutus wore a diaper under his denim shorts outfit.

"Boys," their father said firmly, "I don't want any wild stuff in the house . . . no cartwheeling and somersaults and racing around inside."

They stared back stubbornly at their father, then the instant he turned away, exchanged mischievous glances.

By the time Becky had been given the tour of doors, windows, and fire extinquishers, Emily had the safety checklist filled out and tacked up near the kitchen phone. "There's pizza and carrot sticks for dinner, and brownies for dessert," she said. "Philip and Oliver can show you everything else. All three of them go to bed at eight, but the older boys can read for a while by themselves."

Becky nodded, then glanced at the boys.

Judging by their expressions, they weren't going to follow

bedtime rules or anything else unless she was very clever.

"We'll be back at nine or so," Jeffrey said, hurrying his wife along toward the front door. "Have lots of fun! And, you boys, be good!"

Becky nodded again, then waited to lock the door behind them. She turned to the boys and noticed they stood facing her, ready for trouble. Instead of saying a word, she started for the kitchen.

As they followed along, Philip asked her, "Aren't you going to talk to us?"

Becky shook her head.

"Talk to us! Talk to us!" the two older boys began to yell. "We'll be good . . . we'll be good!"

"No! Won't be good!" Jackmon objected.

"We'll *make* him be good," Oliver promised.

She turned on the oven for baking the pizza, and scrutinized the kitchen to see where everything was. Between the family room and the kitchen, a table was already set for them, and a high chair stood near it.

"We'll be good," the boys promised again.

Maybe she was being too hard on them because of her own troubles, Becky decided. Just because she felt unhappy didn't mean she should be unpleasant with them. Besides, maybe they knew something useful about their great-uncle, Paul Bradshaw.

She took the carrot sticks from the refrigerator. "Why don't you have a few of these?"

"We don't like carrot sticks," Philip announced.

"No!" Jackmon yelled. "Want ice cream!"

Suddenly Philip and Oliver took off, cartwheeling from the kitchen into the family room.

"You're not supposed to cartwheel!" she called after them. Racing behind them, she just barely saved a floor lamp.

Now Jackmon was trying to cartwheel and hit his head on the floor. For an instant, Becky thought he might be knocked out, but he stood right up and tried again.

Philip and Oliver cartwheeled all around the family room and kitchen, and Becky yelled, "Stop this very instant! Stop!"

They ignored her, grinning from ear to ear as they tore around the rooms. *Lord, help me!* she prayed.

Becky guessed that the boys did this often and no amount of yelling would stop them. She stood back and, watching them, said, "You know, you guys are pretty good at gymnastics. Maybe you should go to gymnastic meets like my friend Jess. She does all kinds of gymnastics."

They stopped for an instant.

"What does she do?" Philip asked.

"Everything. Front and backflips, vaults, and stuff on the parallel bars . . . all kinds of gymnastics. She's won lots of trophies and ribbons. I bet if you took some lessons, you could do it, too."

"Why didn't she come today?" Oliver asked.

"Maybe she will next time," Becky answered. "Especially if I tell her you like gymnastics. But she won't come if she hears you're wild and won't mind anyone."

The boys wanted to hear more, and while Becky heated the pizza, she said, "If you're good, I'll draw you pictures of gymnastic equipment . . . you know, parallel bars and a vaulting horse, and gymnastic rings that hang from the ceiling."

"I'll get a tablet for you," Philip said, starting a race to his room.

Whewwww! Becky thought. The Lord had helped her take

a problem and turn it around into something useful.

As the evening wore on, the boys didn't become perfect, but at least they were more agreeable. And they liked to see her draw, especially when she did rough sketches of them.

"I think that's the talent God has given me," she told them, realizing that drawing them calmed her, too. "Maybe He's given you gymnastic talents. Maybe, if you work hard, you could be in the Olympics."

They were definitely interested in that.

At bedtime, she made up stories about their becoming famous gymnasts, pleasing them even more. Their attitudes had changed from being negative and destructive to being positive and creative. If only someone could do that for her!

When their parents arrived at nine o'clock, the boys were asleep. "How did it go?" Mr. Jeffrey Bradshaw asked.

"Pretty well," Becky reported. "They're interested in maybe being gymnasts . . . you know, taking gymnastic lessons."

Mrs. Bradshaw raised her reddish brows. "I'd never thought of it. That would work some of their energy out, too. What a good idea!"

When their father drove Becky home, he said, "Well, well . . . I'm impressed. You're the first baby-sitter in years who hasn't complained about the boys."

Becky had to smile. It seemed that once she'd seen what might be the boys' talents, everything had turned around.

"I hope you'll be happy with your mom's marriage," he added. "My uncle's a great fellow, even though his first wife wanted a divorce. Then, of course, she died instead."

"A divorce?!" Becky echoed. "His wife wanted a divorce?!"

He groaned. "Guess I've been blabbering too much again. Forget that I mentioned it."

No way would she forget it! Becky thought. This was exactly the kind of information she'd been desperate for! Now she really and truly had "something." Something that should stop the wedding!

The moment Becky stepped into the house, she planned to tell Mom the news. But Mr. Bradshaw was sitting with Mom on the living room couch, so Becky decided not to tell her in front of him.

"How was the baby-sitting?" Mom asked.

"All right," Becky answered, hurrying along through the living room.

"I'm glad to hear it," Mr. Bradshaw said. "Those great-nephews of mine can be wild."

You know it, Becky agreed silently. But instead of saying so, she just rushed for the hallway. "Good-night!"

The next morning, she slept late, and Mom had already left for work. As it was, Becky barely made it in time for Morning Fun for Kids.

That evening, as soon as Becky returned from the TCC meeting, she heard Mom on the phone in her room. The minute Mom came into the kitchen, Becky said, "I have something bad to tell you about Mr. Bradshaw. Something terrible."

Mom stopped, her blue-green eyes wide. "What's that?"

Becky decided to come right out with it. "His wife, the one who died, wanted a divorce."

Mom nodded sadly. "I knew that."

"You did?"

Mom nodded again. "She was very ill with cancer, and it affected her brain. Sometimes, when the brain is affected, the person can become very angry. It was very upsetting and a great sadness for Paul."

"I—I didn't know that," Becky answered, staring into space.

"Of course you couldn't," Mom said. She dropped a kiss on Becky's forehead.

"I appreciate your concern, Beck, but you mustn't worry for me."

Becky turned away. She wasn't just worried for Mom; she was worried for their entire family!

"Have you tried on your bridesmaid dress?" Mom asked. She quickly added, "It's in your closet. We want to be sure it fits. It's going to be perfect with your beautiful blue eyes."

It is not-not-not going to look perfect with my blue eyes! Becky thought. Nothing was going to be perfect. She ran to her room, threw herself onto her bed, and cried for a whole hour. What could she do now?

CHAPTER 10

The next few days passed in a blur, and Becky tried harder than ever to forget the wedding. Her TCC friends had already chalked *Hamilton-Bradshaw wedding, 2 to 4,* on Jess's greenboard, but even they didn't discuss it with her anymore.

Then it was Friday night—time for the dreaded wedding rehearsal. As Mom drove their car into the church parking lot, Becky remembered what Bear had told them last Sunday: "It sounds as if you've been crowding Jesus out of your hearts."

She recalled her hurt-filled thought: *It was Mom and Mr. Bradshaw who were crowding Jesus out of her life!*

Here came Gram's car into the church parking lot, and Mr. Bradshaw's dark blue Cadillac pulled in behind her. All three of his sons rode with him. Jonathan would be the best man at the wedding, and Charlie and Quinn would be ushers.

They parked right beside Mom's car, and as they got out, Amanda yelled, "Paw-paw! Paw-paw!"

Mr. Bradshaw grinned. "That's music to my ears, Amanda!"

Quinn rolled his eyes skyward, and Becky couldn't blame him. No way would she ever call Mr. Bradshaw that. *No way!*

Seconds later, Mr. Bradshaw kissed Mom's cheek. She whispered something to him that sounded like "Not in front of the children," then they laughed together.

They liked each other a lot, that much was sure, Becky thought. It was sure, too, that their liking each other made Quinn angrier than ever. Her too!

Gram got out of her car. "Isn't this wonderful? Who'd have ever thought our lives would have taken such a marvelous turn?" She gave Becky a kiss, then Amanda.

"Hold my hand, Gram," Amanda told her.

Something in Becky wanted to hold Gram's hand, too, but she refused to give in.

As they all made their way into the church, she asked Quinn from the corner of her mouth, "Where's Julius?"

"Gone," he muttered. "Gone forever."

"Sorry. . . ."

"I doubt that!" he shot back.

She didn't answer, but she was beginning to feel sorry for him—yes, actually sorry for him, Quintin Bradshaw.

Reverend Meyer met them in the church sanctuary. He was tall, blond, and handsome, and gave them his comical lopsided grin. "Well, bless my bones," he remarked, "if you don't make a fine-looking family."

Mom smiled, and Mr. Bradshaw said, "Thank you, I think so, too. What's more, I've always wanted a big family with a few daughters thrown in."

Another surprise! Becky thought. She paused and studied

his face. It looked like he was telling the truth.

Minutes later, they were practicing what everyone would do during the wedding, even where they should stand. Her job was more important than she'd expected, Becky realized. She'd have to walk down the aisle alone to the organ's wedding music, right before Mom came up the aisle. Then she'd have to give Mom the wedding ring for Mr. Bradshaw—and not drop it. What if she did?!

After the rehearsal, Mom came over to her. "Becky, let's drive to the restaurant together. Amanda is going with Gram."

Suddenly Becky felt shy. "Okay," she mumbled, and walked over to their car.

Once they were inside, Mom didn't start the motor. Instead, she turned in her seat to face Becky. "Are you feeling any better, Beck? Paul and I know it can be hard for kids to face changes, so we expected some resistance. But I've been worried about you. You seem so unhappy, and I've been praying for you."

"For me? I thought you didn't care anymore!"

"What? Of course I care, Becky! You're my precious daughter, and I love you! Nothing could ever make me stop caring for you! I thought you knew that."

"Well, I guess I did, kinda." Becky stared at her shoes. "It's just that I've been so . . . miserable, missing Dad and everything. And it's all happened so fast. . . ."

"Oh, honey, I need my bright and sweet Becky back. I miss her so!"

Becky couldn't answer. A huge lump filled her throat, and she could barely swallow. Suddenly, Mom's arms were around her, holding her tight and squeezing her hard.

After a few moments, Becky tried to joke. "Mom, you're as bad as Julius Squeezer!"

They both laughed.

It felt good to laugh for a change, Becky noticed. But it felt even better to be hugged. Maybe Nana and Gramp Hamilton were right. . . .

When they arrived at the Italiano Grill, a fun restaurant, everyone else was already seated. Lively music filled the huge white stucco room, and college-aged waiters and waitresses, trays held high, rushed around with big smiles.

"We're with the Bradshaw party," Mom told the hostess.

"This way!" The blond hostess led the way to their table, where everyone waited for them. She seated Mom, and Mr. Bradshaw, who'd risen to his feet, asked, "Becky, may I seat you?" His kind gray-blue eyes shone at hers.

She was beginning to like him a little better, she thought. She gave him a nod. "Thank you, Mr. B."

"Well, Becky!" he said. "I think I like being called Mr. B. Is that going to be your name for me?"

Becky nodded again, even though she didn't know how that name had slipped from her lips. "For now, anyway."

Mom and Gram were smiling at her, too.

Calling him "Mr. B." wasn't anything like calling him Dad or Paw-paw, Becky decided. Anyhow, that's what she'd call him—Mr. B.

At dinner, they talked about hilarious happenings at weddings, such as a bride's long train getting caught in the aisle candles, so she couldn't move forward. Well, Mom wasn't wearing a long train on her dress, Becky thought.

Just before awakening the next morning, Becky seemed to hear a small, still voice. *Only you can crowd me out, Becky.*

She blinked, wide awake.

Only you can crowd me out?!!!

Right away, she understood what it meant. She'd been the one who'd crowded Jesus out of her life. She—not Mom or Mr. B., or anyone else. Bear had told them what a no-brainer it was to backslide, to drift away from God.

She remembered the Jeffrey Bradshaw boys and how God had helped her with that "impossible" situation. Then she remembered the song they'd sung at church. Still in bed, she sang it under her breath, "Come into my heart, Lord Jesus . . . come into my heart. . . ." Slowly she began to feel hopeful. Maybe God could turn this into something good for their family, for her.

A bird was singing outside her window, and Becky opened her eyes. God had created that bird—not to mention the sky and the earth and everything else. He'd even given birds wings to fly and songs to sing. So why couldn't He give Mom a new husband . . . and her and Amanda a new father?

Thinking of Mr. B. as Mom's husband and their stepfather seemed more agreeable, Becky decided.

At one o'clock, Becky gazed at her reflection in the mirror behind her bedroom door. Was the girl in the long silk blue dress really her? It did look nice with her blue eyes.

Gram had just settled the halo of white and yellow flowers on her head, making her look slightly angelic. And her white shoes and lace stockings were perfect with the white and yellow flowers in her halo and bouquet.

"Becky Hamilton, you look marvelous," Gram said. Gram looked nice herself in her peach-colored dress, and matching peach shoes and clutch handbag. "Just wait here while I finish with Amanda."

Minutes later, Amanda came into Becky's bedroom to gaze into the mirror with her. She wore a yellow silk dress and matching halo of yellow and white. They stood there in Becky's favorite colors, just like her room: blue and yellow.

Mom arrived to see them. She wore a cream-colored wedding dress that stopped just below her knees, and a halo of creamy flowers rested on her hair.

Becky could feel her lips dropping open. "Oh, Mom, you look beautiful . . . really beautiful!"

"So do you . . . so do both of you. I've always been proud to have you as my daughters, but I especially am now. What's more important, Becky, you don't seem quite so set against my marriage. I've prayed and prayed for God to change your heart about it, and I think I'm getting my sweet Becky back."

Becky's eyes clouded with tears, but she didn't say anything.

"Time to leave for church," Gram told them. "That Paul Bradshaw is getting a very beautiful family."

"So are we," Mom answered. "Quinn's still unsure about it, but he'll come around."

"Let's hurry!" Gram said, and they rushed outside to her car.

Next door, Tricia stood by her mailbox, getting the mail while her family got into the minivan in their garage. They had to go early, too, since Mrs. Bennett was singing in the wedding. Tricia wore her white blouse and skirt, and the TCC medallion around her neck. "Whoa!" she called out. "You all look beautiful!"

Becky beamed. "Hey-hey, as Bear would say. You look nice, too."

"We decided that the TCC girls should wear lace stockings to attend a wedding and serve at the reception."

With her life in such a whirl, Becky hadn't even noticed Tricia's white lace stockings. "They really look great."

For an instant, she wished she would be serving with the Twelve Candles Club at the reception. But she knew she had something more special to do. "See you! See you soon. Just don't do our klutz act at the reception!"

Tricia laughed. "No way!"

The Bennetts' minivan was out of their garage now, and Tricia hurried for it. "We're going to pick up Jess, Cara, and Melanie. We're all invited to the wedding!"

Becky was glad to hear it—and glad that her best friend knew enough not to ask any personal questions right now. Luckily, Amanda was creating a diversion, showing off her yellow dress to Bryan who watched her from the minivan.

Once they were all in Gram's car, the familiar blocks disappeared in a blur. It seemed only moments before they drove up behind Santa Rosita Community Church. They climbed carefully out of Gram's car, then hurried into the back door to the special bridal room, where the bouquets awaited them.

Inside, organ music filled the sanctuary, and Becky said, "It's starting already!"

Mom smiled. "Just the music. We wait here."

Mrs. Meyer, the minister's wife, stuck her head into the bridal room. "How beautiful you all look! Thought I'd stop by to see if you need help."

"We're as ready as we'll ever be," Mom said, excited. "But we'd be glad for you to stay and pray for us."

Mrs. Meyer took their hands, and they all bowed their heads. "Heavenly Father," she began, "you know what an important day this is for this family. We pray for your blessing on this marriage and this family, and for wisdom, peace, and joy . . . and for your wondrous love to shine through all of them during this wedding ceremony and ever after. In the precious name of Jesus we pray. Amen."

It seemed only minutes later that Charlie knocked at the door. "All ready?" he asked as Gram opened the door.

"That we are," Gram said. "Guess I'm first." She turned to the rest of them. "I'll be praying for you as you come down that aisle. You won't have a strong fellow like Charlie to help you along."

She winked at Charlie and took his arm. "Come along, young fellow. It's been a long time since I've had someone so handsome to walk me down a church aisle."

They all laughed, then Mom reminded Amanda about how to scatter the rose petals down the church aisle. "Walk slowly," she told her again. "Don't run."

Amanda stuck her chin out. "I know how. I'm going to practice for when I marry Bryan."

They all laughed, and headed for the hallway that led to the side door by the church's vestibule.

At the door, Mom asked, "Ready, Amanda and Becky?"

They both nodded with a little uncertainty.

The opening chords of the "Bridal March" resounded through the sanctuary, and they hurried into the vestibule. "Time for you to go down the aisle, Amanda," Mom said. "Be sure to smile and to throw the rose petals from your basket carefully."

Amanda smiled brightly and started down the aisle.

Feeling jittery, Becky held the door open a crack to peek out. Glorious music filled the sanctuary, and Mr. B. stood by the altar between Reverend Meyer and Jonathan. They watched Amanda walk down the aisle between the flickering pew candles.

And there was Gram up front, sitting so straight, the sun shining through the stained-glass windows on her. Becky knew she was praying for them.

Amanda scattered the red rose petals gracefully on the white aisle runner. She only skipped toward the end, though she didn't actually run. Finally she climbed into the pew beside Gram.

"Now you, Becky," Mom said, giving her a gentle hug on her shoulders. Her eyes brimmed with love. "Be sure to smile."

Becky swallowed hard and started down the aisle, pasting a smile on her face. She paused in time with the music, but her bouquet shook. *Please, Lord*, she prayed, *don't let me ruin this wedding . . . don't let me trip now, or drop the ring. Most of all, please help me to . . . reflect your love.*

The guests seemed a blur, but they smiled at her as she passed. Then she did see Tricia, Jess, Cara, and Melanie all sitting together and beaming at her.

Her eyes clouded again, and she forced them toward Mr. B., Jonathan, Charlie, and Quinn. For an instant, they all seemed frozen in time: Mr. B. and his sons waiting as she walked up the aisle. Mr. B. smiled at her and, surprisingly, Becky found herself smiling back.

It occurred to her that this was her new family, and God

loved them all. Then suddenly, very suddenly, she began to love them, too. It was so amazing, she felt as if she'd burst with gladness. Stopping in place next to Reverend Meyer, she turned to face the guests and couldn't help smiling joyously.

Seven triumphal notes sounded, and the congregation rose to its feet. Mom came down the aisle slowly, in time to the music. She was smiling and more beautiful than Becky had ever seen her. As she moved down the aisle, her eyes touched on all of them with love, then she focused on Mr. B. Their gaze held so much love that Becky felt her throat tighten with emotion.

Reverend Meyer began the service. "Dearly beloved, we are gathered here in the sight of God and man. . . ."

The wonderful words filled the sanctuary, binding them together into a new couple and a new family. After a while, a man sang "Jesus Is the Cornerstone," then Mom and Mr. B. began to exchange vows, which actually meant promises of love.

In the middle of the vows, Mr. B. sang right to Mom, "Yours Is My Heart Alone," and Becky knew from the way he looked and sounded that he meant it. He really loved her.

After more vows, Mrs. Bennett sang "I Love You Truly."

At last, it was time for Mom and Mr. B. to exchange rings, and Becky remembered to give his ring to Mom. Before long, Reverend Meyer said, "You may now kiss the bride."

Becky watched. This time Mr. B. didn't kiss Mom on the cheek, but right on the lips. Surprisingly, there was something holy about it. A wedding kiss.

Reverend Meyer announced, "Ladies and gentlemen, it is my privilege to present Mr. and Mrs. Paul Bradshaw."

Mom and Mr. B. turned toward the congregation, beaming. Suddenly Becky was holding Jonathan's arm and following Mom and Mr. B. up the aisle. Then they were outside the church and headed for the nearby reception lounge, where even Becky and Amanda were included in the receiving line.

Quinn was right behind her, and Becky wondered what he was thinking. Probably he'd be able to adjust to the changes sooner or later. Becky made up her mind right then and there to be nice to him. If she could change, so could Quinn Bradshaw.

Jess, Cara, Tricia, and Melanie arrived in the lounge in no time, and they looked great in their white outfits with white lace stockings. They headed straight for the lounge kitchen, then were out seconds later carrying trays of tiny sandwiches and cups of punch.

In the receiving line, Gram was first, then Becky, Amanda, and Mom. Mr. B. stood on the other side of Mom with his sons. Quinn looked resigned to the situation, as if he'd given up.

During a gap in the line of guests, Mom told Becky, "I'm so proud of the Twelve Candles Club. They're friendly and they do such a smooth, lovely job."

"I'm proud of them, too," Becky replied. She wasn't going to tell Mom, but her friends had been lots wiser than she'd been about Mom getting married.

Finally, all of the guests had passed through the receiving line, and Mom and Mr. B. were ready to mingle with everyone. First, though, Mr. B. turned to Becky and Amanda. "I'm so glad to have the two of you in our new family."

Love glowed in his gray-blue eyes and, all of a sudden, Becky wanted desperately to hug him. She threw her arms open.

He hugged her mightily. "Oh, Becky! Right now, I can't think of anyone else from whom I'd rather have a hug."

Her eyes clouded up again, and suddenly Jess, Cara, Tricia, and Melanie stood around them smiling and cheering with joy.

"All right, Becky! All right!"

And she knew that—like Jesus and her own family—her friends loved her. Yes, every last one of them in the Twelve Candles Club.